The Night Crew

Brad Ricks

**Published by Crystal Lake Publishing
Where Stories Come Alive!**

**Crystal Lake Publishing
www.CrystalLakePub.com**

Copyright© 2025 Brad Ricks

Join the Crystal Lake community today
on our newsletter and Patreon!
https://linktr.ee/CrystalLakePublishing

Download our latest catalog here.
https://geni.us/CLPCatalog

Cover art:
Christian Bentulan: www.coversbychristian.com

Layout:
Edmund Stone: https://Linktr.ee/edmundstoneauthor

Edited and proofed by:
Jaime Powell, Jodi Shatz, and Monica Camarena

Follow us of Amazon:

WELCOME
TO ANOTHER

CRYSTAL LAKE PUBLISHING
CREATION

Join today at www.crystallakepub.com & www.patreon.com/CLP

To my parents,

Marshall and Debbie Ricks,

For your continued love, support, and encouragement

Prologue

Someone pounded on the front door.

Half asleep on the couch, Brittany White jerked her nodding head up. She'd been lying with her legs stretched across the other seats. Her arm propped her up, and the living room television streamed some Netflix movie she paid no attention to. Background noise.

Mike had called earlier and told her he would be working another late night. He always volunteered for overtime.

After the initial jolt awake, she sat quietly, questioning if she actually heard a knock or if she dreamed it.

Brittany's eyes became heavy as she listened. She caught her head nodding, and the snap of her neck woke her back up. Just as she dozed off again, convinced the noise was a dream, the door rattled from another thunderous hit. The deep tone reverberated through the small house.

Not expecting company at this late hour, she assumed it could only be Mike at the front door.

Finally, he's home.

She walked to the door. "Got off early? Lose your key?" she said to the door, still half-asleep, rubbing her contacts into place.

She unlocked the deadbolt, turning the thumb-latch. The click shot her out of the autopilot routine of unlocking the door, and she grew more awake. It was strange that Mike hadn't called on his way home. She glanced at the clock with her fingers, hesitating on the doorknob latch.

A prickle ran up her spine, but she told herself she was being silly. Mike was always telling her to be careful late at night, but she was so relieved he came home earlier than expected that she unlocked the doorknob. As she did, she realized Mike never responded from outside the door.

Before she could twist the small golden latch on the doorknob back to its locked position, the doorknob turned, disengaging the latch bolt from the door. Brittany pressed her shoulder against the door, bracing it. "Mike, is that you?" she hollered as the pressure on her shoulder increased. "Michael White, if that is you, you better answer me!"

An immediate force on the door threw her back onto the floor, and a figure rushed in. She tried to scream, but a hand tipped with razor sharp nails grabbed her around the throat, catching the scream before it could escape. It tossed her into the middle of the living room. She felt an instant of weightlessness before her back collided with the floor on the other side of the couch. The thing pounced on top of her, ripping at her flesh with its long fingernails, burying them into her side and chest.

Arms flailing, Brittany fought back. She dragged her fingernails across the face and neck of her attacker, but they left no marks. She stared into its burning red eyes, captured by them. She felt searing pain as her blood spilled from her body. Her eyes grew heavy, but this time not from sleep. Darkness began to swallow her. As her vision blurred, she felt lips against her neck followed by a sharp sting.

The darkness grew. Somewhere, deep in the abyss, she heard Michael's voice call out to her. She tried to call for him, ask him why this happened, but nothing came out. Blood coated her throat and flooded her lungs.

1

My name is Michael White, and unlike most people, I know exactly the day I died and why.

I wish I could say I died of old age in my sleep or of a heart attack from eating too much fast food. That would've been simple.

I even wish I could say my passing served some noble purpose. I'd served in the Special Forces and seen a few of my friends die honorably for our country.

The best I could say is I went out fighting. Fighting for my late wife and my new friends.

Welcome to my death.

It started at a funeral, but not my funeral.

Not yet.

2

Just over a dozen people came out for Brittany's funeral in the cool October mist. We didn't have children. No extended family; just us. Both our parents had died a few years ago. That's how we met, oddly enough. Grief counseling.

Sitting by Brittany's casket, I stared into the small patch of rocky Texas earth that would forever be her home. I placed my elbows on my knees and clasped my hands together in prayer. Tears welled up in my tightly closed eyes as I thought back to the first time I met her. I was sitting in a folding chair in a church fellowship hall. Nine of us in a circle. The counselor sat to my right with Brittany two chairs past her. Her fiery red hair contrasted against her ivory white skin. I barely heard a word the counselor said. I stared at the angel with the red halo, trying not to be too obvious but failing miserably. She had me the first time I set eyes on her. In that moment, I saw a spark of Heaven through the darkness. Grief that started when I heard about my parents' accident.

Now, grief held me in its solemn embrace again. What I wouldn't give to be back in that fellowship hall, staring at her three seats down, hoping I didn't seem creepy, instead of where I was now, sitting two feet from her casket.

A tent kept everyone relatively dry, although the wind continued to hit us with mist. Everyone had loved her, but the weather happened to match my mood. Those who braved it mainly stood, avoiding the wet seats.

The minister finished the graveside ceremony. "Receive the Lord's blessing. The Lord bless you and keep you. May He show his face to you and be merciful to you. May He turn his countenance to you and give you peace. May the Lord bless you. In the name of the Father, and of the Son, and of the Holy Spirit." He made the sign of the cross as he spoke.

The dozen who stood around me spoke in unison, "Amen." One by one the mourners grabbed a rose and laid it on her casket. They walked past me, but I didn't get up. I couldn't yet. My head still hung to my chest, hands together in prayer. My eyes stung from the tears.

Dustin, our—no, my next-door neighbor—placed his hand on my shoulder. "Mike, don't forget. Amanda and I are here for you. Let us know what you need."

I nodded in acknowledgment, but I also knew no one would be able to help with what I needed.

Others passed by and said a quiet prayer for me. A friend of Brittany's gave me a hug. Finally, with everyone else gone, the priest sat down in the rain-dampened chair next to me. Beautiful flowers that flanked each side of her casket rocked in the wind but stayed steadfast.

"Mike, please know the Church is here for you," he said gently. "Brittany was, and you are, well loved. If you need to talk about your grief, my door is always open." He placed his hand on my back and said a brief prayer.

"Thank you, Father," I said.

He used that word I hated so much: grief. Grief was something I hadn't needed to be familiar with since I met her. Brit was my salvation. Before college, I served in the Army. I saw my fair share of grief and worked through it. Then, my parents' accident forced me to deal with it again.

Revisiting those infamous stages of grief, I knew I was in Camp Depression. I had cycled through a few of the others already. I firmly stood in Camp Denial while I held her mutilated body that night. She lay dying in my arms, gurgling sounds emanating from the wounds in her chest. Horrible, nightmarish sounds. I heard them but still told her she'd be okay. Even when the gurgling stopped, I continued to tell her everything would be okay. She'd pull through. Denial, party of one.

Camp Bargaining came shortly after. "Please God, take me instead. Let her live and take me," I screamed to the ceiling and beyond. In the distance, I could hear the ambulance sirens.

I visited Camp Anger as the EMTs ran through the door and took her away from me. "Why weren't you here quicker?" I yelled as they forcibly removed me from my house.

As the ambulance pulled away, as I checked myself into a hotel room, I had wrapped myself inside of the numbness of Camp Denial again. Denial worked well, until I meandered over to Camp Depression. That camp was a bitch and didn't want to let go.

Just over a week later, I sat for a few more minutes before finally standing. The wind died down, and the mist finally stopped. I saw four other tents sprawled out across the cemetery. Each guarded mourners from the weather. A man and a woman stood under an umbrella next to the hearse that carried Brittany here. The funeral home van sat parked just beyond it. I assumed they were waiting for me to leave before packing up the chairs, lowering the casket into the ground, and covering her up. I placed a hand on her silver casket.

"I love you, and I miss you," I said, choking back tears. I felt heat rising inside of me. Next stop, Camp Anger. "I'm going to keep my promise."

3

As I strode in the grass toward my car with my head down, I heard a familiar voice. "Mr. White, a moment?"

I peered up and saw Detective John Jennings standing next to my black Acura. He stood as tall as me but had forty pounds of extra mass around his waist. Dressed in blue dress pants and a white long sleeve shirt with the sleeves rolled halfway up, he couldn't look more like a TV detective if he tried.

I continued my way to the car. The saturated ground squished beneath my shoes, so I moved to the gravel road instead, hoping to avoid the worst of it. Unfortunately, the dark brown mud that had already caked to my shoes simply grew a layer of yellowish white powder.

The detective waited by my car instead of meeting me halfway. "Morning, Detective," I called out, still walking to my car.

"Pretty service," he said. I didn't recall seeing him amongst the dozen people under the tent. Over by the car would've been too far to hear anything through the wind and rain.

He's just being polite, I told myself.

"Thanks," I finally replied. "Do you usually attend the funerals?"

"Occasionally." He pulled his phone out of his pocket and started swiping on the screen. "You've given your statement how many times now?"

"Twice at least," I hesitantly replied. The randomness of the question set me back. "The officer that night, and you the next day."

"Yep, that's what I have here. Good. Thanks. Your statement was the same both times also. All good there." John Jennings rocked back and forth on his feet while scrolling through the notes on his phone. He made a few more quick swipes, clicked the button on the side of it, and placed it back in his pocket. "Let's take a walk, Mike. Mind if I call you Mike?" He ventured past my car and stepped on the grass next to the gravel road.

"That's fine." I had to do a quick jog to catch up. To my right, I saw the two from the funeral home packing up chairs.

"Mike, I want to update you so far."

"I appreciate you coming out for Brittany's funeral, but do you think here is the best place?" I asked. The tent that had kept us all mostly dry began slowly coming down. Her coffin remained above ground for now. The grass knocked off some of the white and brown mud from my shoes, but they'd still need to be cleaned later.

He kept walking forward. "As good a place as any. Now, you said the assailant was there when you got home. You told that to me and the officer on the scene." I joined him on his right side and nodded as he spoke. "You fought but he got the better of you."

I glanced in Brittany's direction again. My eyes constantly drew to her casket. Although the cemetery lay flat where we walked, just beyond Brittany's grave rose a hill. The cemetery continued up the side of it, dotted with tombstones. I saw two other tents I hadn't seen earlier. Seven funerals in total on a rainy morning. A slight breeze blew through the trees, taking some of the leaves that had already turned brown with it. It also sent a chill through my damp clothes. The temperature had been falling over the past week. Fall crept in early this year. Unusual for Texas.

I continued to nod in agreement with Jennings. Today was not the day I wanted to relive her death.

"Now, correct me if I'm wrong, Mike; you served in the military. Thank you for that, by the way. Always appreciative of someone who serves his country." He paused a moment. Still staring straight ahead while walking, he continued, "But you didn't just serve. Your service record is quite impressive." The detective's tone changed. A slight arrogance slipped into his voice. I knew he was driving at something and feared I had an idea of what it was. "Actually, you were quite the G.I. Joe bad ass. Special Forces, three tours in Afghanistan. Hell, you have commendations. Now, let me ask you again, just to clarify, you fought, and he got the better of you?"

There it was. I came to a halt. The air left my chest as if I took a punch to the gut. I couldn't breathe. Then I felt the heat rising again in my neck and knew my face started to turn red. Time to visit Camp Anger.

Detective Jennings carried on a few more feet before stopping. He looked straight ahead for a few more seconds, waiting for my response. Slowly, he turned around, and I saw a smug look on his face.

"Your statement, which I've read enough to memorize, is quote, 'When I came in, he was kneeling over her, covered in her blood. I ran at him, but he tossed me out of the way and ran out through the door.' That's what you want us to believe? Your version of the one-armed man we're supposed to look for?"

My fists clenched with rage. I turned my head toward Brittany's grave site. Chairs gone. Tent gone. Flowers loaded into the van. I knew what was next. Next time I looked over, she would be in the ground. I turned back to Jennings.

"How dare you?" I gritted through clenched teeth. Welcome to Camp Anger. Here's your T-shirt. Your cabin is over there. Make yourself comfortable. "How dare you meet me at my wife's funeral and accuse me of killing her." I pointed toward the casket. "She's not even in the ground yet, and you want to stand here and accuse me of doing *that* to her?"

"I see you're angry," he said. Obviously, Detective John had no desire to stop pushing my buttons. He wanted to make me angry. "I want you to clarify your statement, Mr. White. Mike. You've had some time to think about it. Anything you want to add or change?"

One last glance at Brittany. I just barely caught the top of her casket as it fell below the ground. I closed my eyes.

Just breathe, Michael. I gasped. I heard Brittany's voice as if she stood next to me. I knew she really couldn't be there, but God if I couldn't feel her standing over my shoulder whispering in my ear. *Remember your promise to me. Remember what you told me as you held me. Breathe.*

I took a deep breath in. Held it. Exhaled. My hands eased slightly. I opened my eyes and swallowed hard. It felt like spikes traveled down my throat. "That *is* what happened," I emphasized. "Maybe he was doped up or something. The guy was fast and strong as an ox for being as thin as he was. I still have the bruises on my side from where he threw me into the wall to prove it." Breathe in. Hold it. Exhale.

Detective Jennings crossed his arms on top of his protruding stomach. Another breeze blew and carried a strong whiff of Axe body spray with it.

At least we're out here.

Inside an interrogation room with that much body spray? Clear case of torture. I caught myself before I smiled.

Good job, Brittany said.

Jennings still had a few buttons to push. "So, of those commendations you have, which one do you lose for getting your ass kicked by a doped-up junkie?"

My hands clenched tight again, and I closed my eyes. I felt her hand on my shoulder, so soft and delicate, calming me. *Remember.* Breathe in. Hold it. Exhale.

I turned around. I made sure I didn't turn to look at Brittany's grave. I didn't want to see her casket not there anymore. If I saw the casket gone, would her voice leave me? Fear kept me from testing that theory. I started back for my car. "Thank you, again, Detective, for attending the funeral."

"Make sure you stick around town for now, Mike," he yelled as the distance between us grew. "Probably going to have more questions for you."

You and your questions can kiss my ass, I struggled not to say.

My pace quickened until I reached my Acura. I unlocked it, opened the door, and sat inside. I peered down and saw white and brown mud prints on the carpet. Looking back up, I saw Jennings still standing in the same place, arms crossed over his chest. I closed the door, started the car, and placed it in drive. The tires kicked up mud and gravel as I drove through the cemetery gates.

4

I sat in my car in front of the Holiday Inn Express for a few minutes. I'd been staying there since it happened. The police told me I could go back to our house, but there was no way.

The last time I walked in there was three days after it happened. I met an officer in front of my house to be my escort. Standing at the curb, I saw tire marks from the ambulance streaked across the lawn. Police tape blocked the entrance to the porch.

The officer led the way down the sidewalk and up the steps to the front porch. I forced myself to take the two steps up. The officer raised the police tape so I could walk under. The same tape covered the front door as well. The officer opened the front door, pushed aside the tape, and motioned for me to come in.

I stood a moment on that porch. Looking at the front window just to the right of the door, I saw images of that night. It allowed a clear view into the living room. Through that window, I had seen…

My legs fought back against every step on the porch. I needed clothes and toiletries, but to get there meant walking into the house, especially past the living room.

My body felt numb. I willed my legs into motion. When I reached the door, the smell hit me first. The stout smell of bleach and disinfectants lingered in the stale air. The room tasted of it.

I let momentum take me further in. One step in front of the other as I stared at the wall to my left. I saw the entry way closet door. Past the closet, the wall extended out until the opening for the hallway. I kept my eyes on that gap in the wall.

Don't look right, I pleaded with myself.

On my right was the living room. The living room where...

I turned left into the hallway. I took a deep breath, relieved but also ashamed that I didn't look. This visit felt like running a gauntlet. I knew what would be around every corner and dreaded each one. Fortunately, darkness covered the hallway. I knew the pictures that hung on the wall by heart as I passed them. Beach trips, concert selfies, memories. Each one painfully joyful.

The officer walked just in front of me. Obviously, they'd been through my house enough times to know where everything was as well. He opened the door to the master bedroom, and I followed him in. I avoided looking at our bed, using only muscle memory to carry me from the door to our closet. I grabbed some of my shirts and pants from their hangers and quickly deposited them into the suitcase. I didn't care what I grabbed. I just didn't want to turn on the light.

But then, the closet light blazed to life. For an instant, I saw Brittany standing in front of me. I blinked, squeezing my eyes together tight. When I opened them, I realized it was one of her dresses that had been turned awkwardly on its hanger. I spun around, and the officer stood behind me. His hand still rested on the light switch. He must have seen the look in my eyes. "Sorry. Should have said something before I did that," he said.

I grabbed a few more clothes and shoved them into the suitcase before walking over to the master bathroom. Using my arm, I swiped everything from the top of my sink directly on top of my packed clothes. A few things fell with a menacing crack. *Hopefully nothing broke.*

On the way out of the bathroom, I stopped at my dresser. Underwear, socks, and a few pairs of jeans topped the suitcase before I zipped it up.

"Anything else?" the officer asked.

"No, I'm done," I said. I couldn't stand to be in the house anymore.

"Let me get that for you," he said, reaching for the suitcase.

My hand beat him to it. "It's fine. We can go." I left the bedroom and headed back down the hall. I lowered my eyes, avoiding the pictures, but as I turned out of the hallway and into the living room, my shoulder caught the wall. My head sprang up out of recoil before I could stop it.

The living room stood directly in front of me. A monument to our life and now her death. I saw her lying there in the middle of the floor. Couch on one side and love seat on another. Noise emanated from the television; whatever she was watching still played. Her hair spread out like a halo around her head. Blood poured from her chest and neck and traveled down her sides. It spread out from her like a grotesque snow angel.

She was there. I was there. He was there. It was all happening now.

I dropped the suitcase. The officer brushed past me and picked it up, snapping me out of my trance. Only the two of us stood in the house. The TV sat lifeless. The carpet in the middle of the living room showed a faint discoloration.

I ran past the door and into the yard, tearing through the police tape of the door and the front porch. I needed to breathe, and I couldn't inside the house. I stood in the middle of the yard, took a deep breath, doubled over, and threw up the little I had eaten.

5

I snapped myself out of the trance, stepped out of my car, and closed the door. I caught my reflection in the window. The past week had not been good to me. My eyes sunk in from a lack of sleep and too many tears. My hair was good, but with a military style cut, it was hard to go wrong. I had never stopped getting my hair cut short after leaving the Army. Found it easier to maintain that way. I barely ate over the past week, so my suit jacket fit looser than it normally did. I could barely see any linebacker stockiness remaining.

My head hurt. Whether from the change of weather, stress, emotions, or all of the above, I felt the unmistakable vise grip of a migraine tightening around my brain. Instead of heading up to my room, I strode down the street the four blocks to a gas station. I needed Motrin and caffeine.

Leaving the gas station, I took double the prescribed dose and downed it with a Coke. Only a few people stood around me on the streets. The morning rain and now the afternoon chill kept most inside for the day. A strong northern wind blew down the street.

I stood at the streetlight, waiting for my turn to cross. On a pole, someone taped a missing person sign. A young kid. I felt sorry for him and his family. Sure, I'd just left my wife's funeral, but I'd heard there is no pain like losing a child. I couldn't imagine the grief they were going through and wondered what camp they were in. I bet they cycled through them pretty quick. Bargaining with God for a safe return. Angry at the boy if he ran away or with whoever may have snatched him. Denial that this could even happen to them.

Green light. Midway down the next block, I briefly paused. The hairs on the back of my neck tingled. The feeling caught me off guard, almost as if someone watched me. Barely anyone stood on the street, so I knew that wasn't the case, but the feeling persisted. Maybe the overdose of Motrin kicked in quicker than expected on my empty stomach.

I trudged further along, crossing over the next street before the light turned red. Walking city streets. The adult version of Red Light, Green Light. Up ahead, another pole with a missing person sign attached to it loomed. I thought it was for the same kid, but as I got close, I saw it was for a little girl.

A random thought jumped into my head; a ghost story from when I was a kid. Years ago, a handful of kids from a nearby town went missing. The city panicked and instituted a curfew. Parents didn't allow their kids to ride bikes to school. That kind of local overreaction. According to the campfire tale, the disappearances just stopped. Then about a month later, a couple of hikers stumbled upon their bodies in the woods. Of course, the great flashlight moment of any campfire tale must be the finale. The bodies had been drained of all their blood. Back then, it was scary as Hell, but as I grew older, I realized how much horseshit was in the story. Bodies that'd been left out in the woods for a month? No shit there wasn't any blood left. I would be surprised if those hikers could even tell they were human remains.

But, what good campfire story worries about facts?

I dropped my head and let my feet lead the rest of the way. Every town had stories like that. When I was a kid, we used to say it happened in the 70's, but when my grandfather told the story, it happened back in the 50's. Same story, different time just like every great urban legend.

When I finally lifted my eyes, I saw that I was back to the Holiday Inn Express. I went inside and took the elevator up to my room. I trudged forward like a zombie, exhausted and drained. Inside, I grabbed the Motrin and decided an extra dose of numbness wouldn't hurt. My stomach growled, telling me I needed food, but I wasn't in the mood. I pulled the curtains over the window as close together as I could to block out the afternoon's waning sunlight. The cloud cover helped as well. I dropped the room temperature as low as it would go and fell into bed. Chilly autumn afternoon after burying my wife sounded like a great time to go to bed. I prayed I would find sleep quickly.

I wasn't that fortunate, though.

I lay in the bed staring up at the ceiling. I closed my eyes, hoping for sleep, but the memory of flashing red and blue lights found me instead. A half dozen police cars blocked off my street from both directions. An ambulance parked in the front yard, the back of it facing my house.

Onlookers stood across the street. The neighbors I've grown to know over the past few years watched and wondered what happened. I skimmed the faces in the group, recognizing most of them. Bob from three houses down stood next to Roy from across the street. Amanda next door talked to Dustin, who stood next to a tall, thin brunette and a large, muscular Black man I didn't recognize. Police lights bring out the curiosity in everyone.

In the memory, I turned away from the crowd hearing commotion at the front door. Two paramedics pushed the gurney through with a black bag on top of it. My Brittany was inside there. I couldn't see her, but I knew. I knew. I ran toward them screaming.

Sirens went off; the sound grew louder and louder.

I hit the alarm on my phone, turning it off. I slowly opened my eyes to sunlight peeking through the curtain. Another day.

6

The shower flowed hot, hotter than I usually like it, but I wanted the heat and the steam. I wanted to bring myself out of Camp Depression.

While drying myself off, my cell phone rang. I rushed over to it, saw the name, and answered. "How do you stop a Syrian tank?" I asked.

"You shoot the guy pushing it, of course," came the answer.

"Austin Jeffries, you sonofabitch, how've you been?" I forced out, trying to sound upbeat but probably failing.

"Better than you. I heard about Brittany. Man, I'm sorry I didn't make the service. Have the police told you anything?"

"Based on what the detective said yesterday, I'm pretty sure he thinks I did it. How'd you hear about it all the way up in DC?" I could hear a keyboard clicking on the other end. In my head, I saw Austin already sitting in front of his computer, sipping his morning coffee.

"Military intelligence, my friend. If I told you, I'd have to kill you."

"Military intelligence is a contradiction in terms. Still don't know how a brain-dead grunt who barely knew how to drive a tank ended up on the intelligence side of things," I shot back.

Austin and I met in Afghanistan on my first tour. We became good friends and stayed in contact. He only lived about an hour away from me when he wasn't stuck in Washington, D.C.

"Mike, I am really sorry. You know I'm here for you. You have a lot of friends if you ever need us." He paused, and I heard him sip his coffee. My stomach growled in jealousy. "I know you didn't do it. That cop must have his head up his ass. What do you think? Robbery gone wrong or something else? You have the best gut I've ever seen."

"My gut feeling? No, this was something else. The guy was definitely doped up, but I can't help but think there's something else going on." My gut twisted in knots as I told him.

"Did you tell the detective everything?"

"Of course."

"Mike, don't bullshit me. Did you do your thing?" he asked.

"No, I didn't do 'my thing.'"

"So do that meditation crap you do and play it again in your head. I know you've been avoiding it. It's going to hurt but do it for her. Slow it down. Use that thing you have. What do you call it? An idiotic memory?"

"It's called an eidetic memory." I knew where he was going.

"Eidetic. Idiotic. Whatever. As soon as we get off this call, do it and tell the detective anything else you find. How many times has your gift saved yours or someone else's ass? Why do you think I've been trying to recruit you since you got out?"

"I thought it was because you needed someone to make you look good," I retorted.

"Yeah, there's that. But you're like a goddamn Sherlock Holmes when you want to be. Put it to good use. For her. You know I love you, Mike. Call me when you need me."

We said our goodbyes and hung up.

I knew what Austin meant to say. The common term was eidetic memory, but that wasn't my only gift.

"He remembers things so vividly," my mother told the doctor. Eight-year-old me sat on the examination table while the doctor listened to my heart. My mother sat in one of the chairs in the small room.

After a thorough examination and a few tests, the doctor left for almost an hour. When he came back, he had a handful of printed pages in his hand. "Well, Mike has what's called Highly Superior Autobiographical Memory. HSAM for short. It is extremely rare. People with an eidetic memory, what people usually call a photographic memory, can remember images perfectly after only glancing at them. We've known Mike could do that. But what makes him even more special is that he can recall events with near perfect recollection. That's HSAM. His brain stores things differently than everyone else."

I had told Detective Jennings what happened, but I didn't "put myself under" as my unit called it. I recalled it like anyone else, but I didn't relive it. Why would I want to? Like I told Austin, though, my gut felt there was more. Unfortunately, he was right. There had to be a detail I missed. Something I could use to find the bastard who killed Brit and make good on my promise to her. Once I was through with him, whatever was left, the cops could have.

I began the routine I learned years ago. For my own sanity, I had to learn how to suppress and control my gift. As a kid, reliving certain events over and over again turned into torture. I could only recall being bullied in middle school or hazed as a high school freshman so many times. I loved remembering the good times, the new bike from Santa, my first make-out session on a blanket in the bed of my truck, but it's surprising how many traumatic events one can have. My head remembered them all. All but one, actually. My friend, Martin, was killed when I was ten. The authorities and my parents told me I was there, but I don't remember. When I've tried to recall the memory, all I got was darkness, as if a recording had been erased.

I went over to the curtains and shut out the sliver of light trying to come through. The air conditioner blew at its coldest already. I sat on the floor, my back against the side of the bed, and crossed my feet in front of me. I placed my hands on my knees and closed my eyes. My breathing slowed as I relaxed my body into the depths of my consciousness. I felt myself slipping into the memory as one slips into a dream. Fortunately, dreams aren't typically real. I fell back into myself as I...

7

I step onto the first, then the second step of the front porch. Does she ever remember to turn the porch light on? I always remember for her, but she never does the same. I really need to put those on a timer, so she doesn't have to remember. The lights will welcome me home each night.

I glance to my right and see the bushes in front of the house. Definitely need to trim those this weekend, assuming I don't decide to pull a weekend shift. I hate working all the hours right now, but that overtime check is great.

My foot lands on the concrete porch.

The blinds are open, and I can see the living room light is on. We never close the blinds. If anyone has a fetish of watching two people sit on a couch and watch Netflix, then they can have at it. It's nice in December, though, when we have the Christmas tree in front of the window. I love being able to see it from the road. In another month, I'll have it up. Sorry, Thanksgiving.

With the living room light on, at least I can see my keys. I stride over to the window with keys in hand, fiddling with them, looking for the one for the front door. My gaze drifts up from the keys, through the window, and into our living room.

What the hell!

Brittany lay in the middle of the living room. The front of her pajamas is torn. A pool of blood in the carpet masquerades her red hair. Her arms twitch and legs flail. Her skin has become a sickly white color.

I drop the keys in my hand and run to the door. I ram my shoulder into it, expecting it to be locked but it isn't. The door bursts open and slams into the wall behind it. Immediately, the room feels cold, as if the life of the house has been drained.

I don't know what to expect, but it isn't what I see. My initial thought that she had slipped and hit her head vanishes when I see him. As the door hits the wall, he stares up at me. He is kneeling over Brit, his face covered in blood. Her blood. His eyes appear to blaze red like the fires of Hell. But that fire is cold, and the empty cold of his eyes resonates through me. The tips of his long, brown hair drip red droplets of blood. Her blood.

My body freezes for an instant. The stare of the stranger... the attacker— her attacker—freezes me in place for a split moment. I almost feel his presence wanting me to stay and wait for him to finish, but I see Brit's leg spasm. She's still alive. I rush toward him and deliver a knock out upper cut.

But I miss. He bends backward as my fist passes millimeters from his face. How did he bend like that so fast? That punch should have broken his jaw and sent him collapsing. Before I have time to reset myself, he's on his feet.

I rush forward, planning to put him back on the ground. My hands make contact with his shoulders. With my body weight, I'm taking him to the ground. When I have him on there, I don't plan to stop punching until he stops breathing.

He places his right hand on top of his left shoulder. There's an emblem on his hand. I know that emblem, a faded cluster of stars, barely visible. It's Club Starlight. I have just enough time to make that realization before he spins me around, redirecting my entire body weight. He throws me across the couch and into the wall.

I briefly see my own stars as my head hits the wall. When my eyes refocus, I no longer see him in the room. In the moment it takes for me to regain my senses, he leaves. Damn, he is fast and strong. I reach into my pocket and pull out my phone, dialing 9-1-1 faster than I've ever typed before.

8

I took a big, deep breath and opened my eyes back up. I had to leave that memory before I walked over to her. I couldn't do that again. Couldn't watch her die in my arms again.

Instead of crying over the past, I focused on the present. I had what I needed for now.

Club Starlight.

9

A new energy swept over me. I felt renewed inside. If Detective John Jennings wasn't going to be of any help, then I'd find Brittany's killer myself. I was glad Austin called and that I had taken his advice. I'd completely forgotten about the faded mark on the guy's hand. With this, I had something to go on.

I set my priorities in order: clothes, food, and then hunting. Tonight was going to be a long night.

I shoved on a pair of jeans and an old Aerosmith T-shirt, donned a baseball cap, and left my hotel room. Meg's Diner sat on the other side of 3rd St across from the hotel. It was a small hole-in-the-wall diner. I jogged across 3rd while my stomach grumbled in anticipation. I hadn't eaten anything but Motrin since yesterday.

Only a few cars sat in the parking lot.

Good, it wouldn't be too busy.

Although I doubted I knew anyone inside, I still couldn't shake the lingering feeling that people were staring at me. Stupid, I know, but it was there.

When I opened the door to Meg's, a bell at the top of the door announced my arrival. The smell of bacon and sausage on the griddle hit me in the face. Immediately, I could feel how long it had been since I ate last.

"Grab a booth anywhere," the older lady behind the counter said in a gravelly voice. Years of cigarette smoking had done her no favors. She wore an apron around her waist that held straws, a notepad, and a pencil. A hair net hugged her scalp, keeping the gray hair prisoner inside.

I glanced around the small diner and found it empty. I guess the staff owned the few cars in the parking lot. To my right was a bar with stools. Across from the bar, a couple of booths lined the exterior wall. The diner had a few tables on my left with a couple of booths against the front there, too. I veered to my right, past the bar, and sat in a booth at the far end with my back against the wall, facing the door. Old habit, always be able to see the exit.

The older lady, Doris according to her name badge, walked over to me with a pot of coffee. She turned over the coffee cup already on the table in front of me and poured without asking. I was grateful. Coffee sounded great.

"Need a menu or know what you want?" she asked.

"Pancakes." I'd never been here before but assumed they'd have pancakes.

"Sausage or bacon? And how do you want your eggs?"

"Both and scrambled," I answered.

She made a note and left without saying anything else. I watched her go past the register to the window and stick the note to a silver clip before spinning the turnstile halfway around. A hand grabbed it away. The chain restaurants may hire nicer staff—and prettier—but there was something nostalgic and comforting about a greasy spoon. I guessed that nothing on the menu would be healthy, or vegan, but couldn't care less.

Sitting in the stiff booth, I sipped my coffee. Black, hot, and about two steps away from tar. Just the pick me up I needed to get my head on right. I missed Brittany, but I needed to push that into its own box. I made her a promise and I intended to keep it. That useless detective had no intention of doing anything but question me, and I could use some retribution over justice.

It wasn't long before I emptied my coffee cup, and Doris walked around the counter with the pot. Without saying a word, she poured another cup and meandered back to her perch. I stared out the window on my left for a while, enjoying my second cup of tar. The bitterness reminded me of the military.

Before I could get too distracted, I heard a clink on the table. Doris set down my plate of pancakes, sausage, bacon, and eggs. "Need anything else?" she asked.

"Syrup and Tabasco would be great."

She reached over to the empty booth in front of me and grabbed them. She resumed her post behind the counter.

To say I ate my breakfast would be an understatement. I was more surprised the plate didn't end up in my stomach as well. Doris filled my cup again midway through. There's nothing better than unhealthy diner food. The nearly burnt bacon and the sausage that sat in grease, filled my stomach past full. I felt a moment of peace for the first time since coming home that night. Whether it was because of the food or because of the mission in front of me—or both—I wasn't sure.

Across the street, I saw the hotel. Cars filled the parking lot. I was lucky to have gotten a room. I saw people coming and going. Strangers all temporarily living feet from each other. The stories a hotel could tell would probably make a prostitute blush.

A couple sat at the bus stop across the street just outside of the hotel. I briefly glanced at them before looking away. Then my gaze shot back to the bus stop. "How do I know them?" I said to no one.

The woman, Caucasian, fairly thin with long brown hair pulled in a ponytail, sat back against the bench, her head turning left and right, pausing occasionally to look straight ahead. The muscular Black man sitting next to her also had his back against the bench. One arm stretched out across the back of it, disappearing behind the woman. He could pass for Terry Crews's stunt double. He appeared to be looking straight ahead at the diner.

By high school, I learned the best way to use my gifts. For the HSAM, I needed to make everything dark and cold, drifting into a meditative state. But for the eidetic memory, I built my own Internet. The ultimate intranet. My Ultranet.

I leaned back in the booth and closed my eyes, imagining myself in an empty room. Four walls, no door. Bookshelves filled with books took shape. It was for ambiance more than anything else. It wasn't like I walked over and grabbed a book. A desk with a wide screen monitor appeared in the middle of the room. I sat at the desk and started typing. As I typed, the contents on the screen filled with pictures, constantly shuffling and updating with every new addition. The images changed in real time. Flashes appeared and disappeared faster than an eye could make them out.

Everything happened in a matter of seconds if not quicker. The images zoomed past and then suddenly stopped as quickly as they started. I found them.

Doris came and took my plate, leaving the bill. I opened my wallet and dropped a few bills on the table. She hadn't peppered me with small talk and kept my coffee cup full, so I left a generous tip. I slid out of the booth, told her thank you, and opened the door. The bell sounded again as I left out of Meg's Diner.

10

I thought about taking the short stroll across 3rd and disappearing back into the Holiday Inn. If tonight goes well, it could be a long night. Since I'd probably be up late, a mid-morning nap wouldn't be a bad idea. And with a full stomach, I'd probably actually sleep soundly.

I also contemplated walking over to the couple at the bus stop. I'd seen them twice already. Standing across the street from my house as my wife's body was loaded into the ambulance, and at her graveside service. They loaded up the chairs and tent. They could've been neighbors who also happened to work for the funeral home. Coincidences did happen. Just because they happened to be sitting at a bus stop downtown in front of my hotel staring in my direction as I ate breakfast didn't mean anything. I felt my paranoia getting the better of me and needed to stop.

Again, no one is following you.

It was just before noon, and the temperature was unusually low for October in Texas. The north wind blowing through the buildings downtown helped to add to the chill in the air. Instead of taking a nap or interrogating random strangers, I opted to head to the store to pick up a few things. Plus, a nice walk would help clear my mind. I headed left from the diner and walked down 3rd St.

I passed Franklin Ave, Jay St, and Jefferson Ave. This part of downtown liked to name their streets after founding fathers. Yesterday, I passed these streets on the other side heading for the Motrin. The traffic light poles had the same missing persons posters on this side. I could hear the wind rustling the pages of them as I walked past.

On Jefferson Ave, I turned left. The nearest grocery store sat just over a half mile away on 7th and Jefferson. Not a bad walk with the cool breeze at my back. Usually, my lunch break would be coming up. I wasn't used to seeing this part of the day. Working in a warehouse didn't offer much change of scenery. Miller's told me to take as much time as I needed away from work. Who knew how long it would take me to exact a little retribution of my own? Work would just get in the way, right now.

I crossed over 4th street. A glass wall filled the block on my left, and I glanced at my reflection. I looked different today than yesterday. I didn't know if it was the way I walked or how I held myself. Something was different. The hardest week of one's life could do that.

Something caught my eye in the reflection. A block back and on the opposite side of Jefferson Ave, the couple from the bus stop trotted down the road. Coincidence? My faith in coincidences eroded.

One way to find out.

I made a left turn at the light on 5th St. This put me heading back in the direction of my hotel. They would have to cross Jefferson to catch up with me.

I quickened my pace, immediately making another turn down a small alley connecting 5th and 4th. I doubled back to 4th St. Before stepping into the open, I placed my back against the brick of the building to my right and eased my head to the side. I could see Jefferson Ave.

My two "neighbors" weren't where they should've been. I darted out of the alley, making a right on 4th. I surveyed the area. Store fronts lined 4th Street on both sides. Cars parked along the road next to parking meters. The four lanes of 4th Street sat quiet with little traffic. I saw a loading truck midway in between Jefferson and Jay St. My training kicked in.

Shuffling to the front of the truck, I walked on the street before slipping under the bed of the truck, hiding in the shadow. Only a few people walked down 4th with others sitting outside at an eatery two stores down. I watched the sidewalk.

"I'm going nuts," I whispered to myself. Brit murdered and now this? I had to be paranoid. With the ground warm and no breeze under the truck, sweat started to slide from my forehead and down my nose. I saw a few droplets hit the road underneath my face.

Two sets of shoes popped out of the alley. The bottom of the truck blocked my view of their faces, but the clothes matched. Their torsos became just jeans and then shoes as they neared the truck. The shoes drew closer, barely a few feet from me. I held my breath. The feet twisted to the right, then back to the left.

They are looking for me.

"Think he made us?" I heard a deep voice say from above.

"No, love," came a female's voice in a heavy Australian accent. "He probably suddenly had to take a shit and ran into a store. I told him, the guy is smart."

"Jax is going to be pissed," the baritone responded.

"I'll deal with Jax. White'll have to go back to his hotel at some point. Nothing's going to happen during the day, anyway. Silas is sleeping."

"Call Jax, and then let's eat. I'm starving."

Then, the shoes turned to Jay St and back down 4th. I slowly released my breath. The sweat dripped off my face onto the pavement below me. The shoes grew jeans, torsos, and finally heads. They crossed 4th and drifted completely out of sight.

My head spun. I crawled out from under the truck, keeping my eyes trained on the direction they traveled. Holy shit! I wasn't being paranoid. I was being followed! I brushed off my hands, shirt, and pants while I maneuvered back to the alley. I took a more indirect route to the store.

Who are those two? Who's Jax? And who's Silas?

11

My wife was murdered a week ago, and now I was being followed.

I went back up Jefferson Ave on the right side of the road. My head constantly stayed on the move. I stared past the cars to people walking across the street, examining the faces of those around me. The glass window of the building on my right was my rear-view mirror.

I opened my senses to take in everything around me. The sounds of engines revving, tires braking, and people talking enveloped me. The air smelled and tasted of exhaust smoke. It was easy to be distracted with so many questions. I used the surroundings to stay out of my own head. If I lost focus, the Australian chick and the Black guy could sneak up on me. Not happening.

Instead of turning down 3rd and going straight back to the hotel, I went two more blocks down. By the time I was at 1st, the midday traffic had increased substantially. First was usually a very busy street. By five o'clock, it was a parking lot.

I turned right and walked until I stood directly behind the Holiday Inn. A fence blocked the way to the parking lot. I hopped on top of a dumpster that butted up against the fence and peered over the side. No stalkers from here. The parking lot sat lower than the fence line, but I jumped over, anyway. I braced myself for the impact, softening my knees when I landed. A quick jog to the back entrance, and I slipped into the building. I raced up the stairs to the 3rd floor and escaped into my room.

Finally, alone with my thoughts, I took the time to think through everything. I grabbed the notepad off the desk in the room and started writing.

Jax. Silas. Club Starlight. Australian woman. Black guy. Being watched. Why? Who are these people? About Brittany's death?

This all started after Brittany was killed. The couple were outside of my house that night. Why were they there? Had they been following me since then? I've been in Camp Depression for the better part of the week. No wonder I never saw them before.

The clock read "2:00 PM" in bright red digits. The club didn't open until 8. My goal was to get there closer to 10 when more of the regulars showed up.

Looking at the notepad, I tore off the first page with my random thoughts on it. On the next page, I started writing out the guy's description. I closed my eyes and pulled him up in my Ultranet. Every last detail.

12

Club Starlight sat on the north side of town just before the city limit sign. The building used to be a warehouse. I remembered the cargo vans staked out front, ready to be filled. During the recession, it sat abandoned until it finally sold to some firm that turned it into Club Starlight. A few other warehouses stood around it, but those remained empty.

I pulled into the parking lot at the front of the club and parked my car. The neon logo, a shooting star with smaller stars underneath it, shone bright above the door which sat in the middle of the building. An awning hung just underneath the sign. The rest of the building still looked like the warehouse it once was. It stood two stories tall, gray, with windows close to the roof. Except for the neon sign and the parking lot lamps, Club Starlight looked like another empty building.

A line of people stood outside of the club, waiting for their turn to go inside. The people wore a random assortment of casual and dressed to impress. Most were in their mid-twenties. I took my place in line, wearing dress jeans, a T-shirt, and a light jacket. Not too casual but nothing fancy. The line moved fairly quickly. While the bouncer checked ID's, a cashier took everyone's cover charge and stamped their hand. The same stamp I saw on Brit's murderer.

I watched for John and Jane, the anonymous couple. My supposed neighbors who were also mortuary assistants and stalked unsuspecting widowers downtown. I didn't see them outside of the hotel when I left, and so far, I hadn't seen them here, either.

As I got closer to the door, I could hear music blaring. Low thumps from the bass reverberated the walls. If it was this loud outside, the inside would be deafening.

Or maybe I am just getting old.

My turn at the door finally arrived. I handed over my driver's license to a tall guy with bulging biceps. He briefly glanced at it and handed it back. Next, I paid my $10 cover charge to the twenty-something-year-old girl behind the counter in tight blue jeans and a low-cut top. I held my hand out. She took it, turned it over, and stamped the top of it. I looked at the stamp that matched the neon sign on the outside of the building. I stepped out of the way and paused for a moment.

Just breathe, Brittany whispered in my ear. I felt her hand on my shoulder again.

I took a deep breath and entered Club Starlight.

13

Strobe lights flashed to the beat of the music. A thick haze of smoke filled the air. At the front of the club, the DJ booth towered above the dance floor. A huge screen filled the wall behind the DJ with images of random shapes and colors, fluidly moving and pulsating in rhythm. High above the dance floor, canisters hung from the rafters, sending dancing rays of light beaming down to the floor.

The bar was situated in the middle of the club. Booths lined the exterior walls, and tables spotted the half of the room that wasn't the dance floor. Mirrors circled the walls above the booths making the room seem to go on eternally. In the infinite reflections, the lights above twinkled like stars in the night.

I swam through the swarm of bodies in front of me, trying to feel my way forward toward the bar. The air sat thick in my lungs with the smoke. I could taste the acidic mixture of machine-made fog and cigarette smoke. Once upon a time, when I was in my early twenties, I spent way too much time in places like this. It was an easy way to numb the images and memories in my head when I couldn't control them.

A crowd of people stood around the bar. Although the jacket felt good outside, I regretted wearing it. All the warm bodies pressed together raised the temperature an easy twenty degrees. I patiently waited through person after person ordering drinks like Shiner Bocks, Tito's and Coke, and a Jack and Dr. Pepper. Finally, I placed my arms on the top of the bar.

"What can I get you?" the bartender asked. He was skinny and stood six inches taller than me with short blond hair.

"Let me get a Shiner," I said and handed over my credit card.

"Opening a tab?" he asked as he walked toward the cooler of beer.

"No, just the one," I shouted back. "Hey, how often are you here?"

"Almost every night. Why do you ask?"

"I'm looking for someone who was here the other night. If I told you what he looked like, do you think you could tell me if you've seen him?"

"I see a ton of people, man," he answered.

"I think he'd stand out."

"Sure. Give it a try."

I briefly closed my eyes and pulled up the image of the piece of paper in my pocket. I read off what I wrote earlier. "Long, curly brown hair. About as tall as you. Thin. His cheek bones stand out high on his face. Cheeks sunken in."

He placed the beer in front of me. "That's it?" he asked.

"Yeah, unfortunately."

"Couldn't tell you, man. Probably described two dozen guys who've been here today."

I signed the credit card receipt he slid over to me and placed my credit card back in my wallet. "Thanks, anyway." I grabbed my beer and moved away from the bar.

Across from the bar, a booth opened up. I scurried over before anyone else noticed it empty. As I scooted into the horseshoe shaped seat and slid to the midpoint, I could see the entrance to the club and a large portion of the dance floor. A waitress in a short skirt and tight shirt came over to me.

"Need anything?" she asked.

I pointed to the beer. "No, thanks. Maybe in a little bit."

I scanned the faces of people as they came into the bar. I watched for the double Does, and I watched for Brittany's killer. With every face I saw, I tried to access my Ultranet as quickly as possible. With the strobe lights of the club constantly pulsating, the faces flashed in front of me. Some shone bright when the light flashed, followed by the instance of darkness.

My gaze darted back and forth. I glanced up where the canister lights were secured to give my head a break. A second story area sat high above the entrance, just above the layer of smog. Management offices that allowed those in charge to keep an eye on the floor.

"Would you like another?" the waitress asked.

I picked up my beer to take another drink and found it empty. I had mindlessly sipped it away while focused on those coming and going out of Club Starlight. The rhythm of the music and the pulsating lights were hypnotic.

"Sure," I answered. "Hey, how often do you work here?"

"Sorry, hon, you aren't my type," she responded.

I laughed. She was easily fifteen years younger than me. "That's not why I'm asking. I'm looking for someone who was here the other night." I proceeded to give her the description I'd given the bartender earlier.

"He sounds familiar," she said. "I think I've seen him around, but I don't know his name. I'll be right back with your beer." She left with my credit card. I guess I should've opened a tab.

Some progress at least. I wasn't completely insane. Someone had seen him before.

Maybe.

She brought back another Shiner, and I signed the credit card slip. I took a swig and went back to people watching.

"Hey, babe. You want to have a good time?" I heard a voice say from the booth next to me.

I turned that direction and saw a young girl. Twenty-one was the age limit to get in and she couldn't have been a day older than that. She had dirty blonde hair cut to her shoulders. The bangs were twisted into tiny braids. She looked like she hadn't eaten in days; a skeleton barely wearing skin. Around her neck, she wore a black and red choker.

"No, thanks," I responded.

She reached her arm over and tossed a pill on the table. "That one's on the house. I've got a whole assortment. What's your poison?"

I pushed the pill aside. "No, thank you," I said again.

She turned around, leaving me with the pill on the table.

I grabbed my Shiner and downed two big gulps. Whether it was the beer, the music, or the long day, I started to feel exhausted. Although the waitress thought the description sounded familiar, she didn't know for sure. I hadn't seen John or Jane. I still had no idea who Silas and Jax were. It was time I went back to the hotel.

After sliding out of the booth, I grabbed the bottle with the remainder of my beer and started to leave out the front door. Immediately, my table filled with people who'd been standing up.

No turning back now.

I waded my way back through the smoke and the waves of partiers until I felt a tap on my shoulder. My first thought was Brit getting my attention again, but then it continued. Turning around, I had to peer down to see the young drug pusher.

"I'm sorry. I'm looking for a person, not drugs," I told her.

"Who are you looking for?" she asked. "I know everyone here."

"I don't know his name, just what he looks like."

"Tell me," she said. "Might be surprised."

What the hell. I told her the description of Brittany's killer. When I finished, I emptied the rest of the bottle down my throat.

"Hey, that sounds like Silas," she said.

I nearly spit out my beer. My heart stopped. Despite the noise in the club, everything went silent in my head. The name Silas echoed in my ears shutting out everything else.

"Where's Silas?" I choked out.

She tossed her head from side to side. I stood a good foot over her so there was no way she actually looked around. People stood shoulder to shoulder.

"Silas? He's not here," she said smiling. Her body swayed back and forth to the beat of the music. "But, hey, see those two guys leaving? They're friends of his." She kept bouncing as she talked.

"Which two?"

She pointed again. "Those two. The one in the leather jacket with black hair, and the hot guy in the short sleeve shirt with a bald head."

I saw who she pointed to and bolted in their direction. The two guys left the club and turned left. I rudely pushed past people and finally finished swimming upriver.

The brisk air hit me as I stepped outside. The two men walked to the end of Club Starlight and turned left, heading to the back of the building. I slowly passed the line of people waiting to enter and followed them. I didn't want to rush into anything. I had no idea who would be waiting for me when I turned the corner.

I moved close to the building as I approached the alley. My hand rested against the cinder block. I stopped and took a deep breath. Suddenly, someone thrust my head into the side of the wall. It exploded with pain. I fell to my knees and doubled over. My eyes lost focus, and stars erupted into my vision. I rolled onto my back and stared up. A figure stood over me. As my eyes regained their focus, I first saw his long, brown hair followed by his gaunt figure. The ghost of my nightmare found me.

My head swam with disorientation, and I realized I was helpless as Silas stood over me.

14

"Pick him up," Silas hollered to the men I followed.

I felt an arm go under each of mine, my body hoisted in the air. The pair dragged me around to the back of Club Starlight and tossed me against the side of the building like a rag doll.

My head felt heavy on my neck. I looked like a bobble head trying to hold it upright. Everything in front of me kept going in and out. After a few attempts, I finally saw clearly enough to examine the situation.

The guy with the leather jacket held me up by my left arm and Baldy had my right. Silas stood in front of me.

"Did I do good, Silas?" came a voice from around the building. I recognized that voice instantly. The skeleton-with-skin drug pusher from inside the club came running around the corner. "Did I?"

"Yes, you did great," he responded. His voice was oddly soothing, silk flowing through the air.

"Do you think I could have one of your special kisses?" she asked. "Please?" She bounced and swayed as she talked. Her hands clasped in front of her, begging him.

"Only since you did so well."

She cheered and clapped her hands together. She brought her arms behind her head and untied the choker she wore. Underneath the choker, bruises and scratches blotted her neck. No amount of makeup would cover that up.

My initial thought was she must be in an abusive relationship. Then I saw Silas stand in front of her, and my whole world changed in an instant.

She tilted her head to one side. Her blonde braids drooped across her shoulder. Silas took his hand and gently brushed the side of her face. He brought his hand down to her neck and caressed it with the back of his fingers. Using the nail on his pinky finger, he made a quick motion, and I saw a line of blood trickle from her neck. The line was dark, almost black in the low-lit alley. It contrasted against the sickly, mottled whiteness of her skin.

Silas raised his head up and violently brought it down on top of her neck. He held her close, arms wrapped around her tiny body. Her arms extended limp to her side. Her face smiled as if she was in pure ecstasy. At one point, I saw her eyes roll back in her head.

I struggled against Leather Jacket and Baldy. I knew Silas was killing her, but I couldn't break free. I was pinned against the wall. They laughed at my failed attempts to struggle.

Silas raised his head and steadied her on her feet. She staggered back a few steps before regaining her balance.

"Cover yourself back up and go back inside," he told her.

She grabbed her choker and tied it around her neck again, covering up the new mark he left. She turned to leave and had to steady herself again. Anyone who saw her would think she was drunk. She placed her hand on the brick wall. Before she turned the corner, she turned around and waved, then disappeared around the front of the building, leaving me with the three men.

Silas turned his attention to me, still a prisoner against the wall.

Since Brit's murder and my promise, I thought frequently about the moment I would find her killer. The revenge I would get. Vengeance for her. My heart sank in my chest with hopelessness and disappointment now. Her killer stood a few feet from me, and I was helpless to do anything. I failed in my promise of vengeance. I at least found solace knowing I would soon join Brittany again.

Stay calm and breathe, her voice said in my head. *This may not be the end yet.*

I stopped struggling, using her voice to steady myself. I firmly planted my feet, although I was still pinned to the wall.

"Been waiting a long time to see you again," Silas said. He stepped a foot closer to me. His lips were still bright red from the blood.

I quickly searched my Ultranet for him. Brittany's murder but nothing else. "Fuck you, you son of a bitch. Big man, you are. You kill my wife, prey on helpless girls, and have to have two of your friends hold me down. Scared to take me on alone? I don't know what a long time for you is, but a week is long enough for me."

"Mike, I love the bravado," he said patiently. The silk of his voice resting upon my ear. He paced in front of me. His long brown curls dancing around his head. "You hold such anger for me. I've come to set you free. Soon, you will be able to experience the world like few others. The smells, the sounds, the lights. You will thank me."

"You're crazy," I countered. "You've lost your fucking mind." I tried to move my arms again, but still couldn't. Damn, they had a tight grip.

He stopped in front of me and brought his face within inches of mine. I could smell the stench of his breath, as if death and decay spewed from it. His eyes stared into mine. They weren't red at all but almost black. He took a step backward and stood back up straight.

Silas turned away from me, looking at the building behind him. When he turned back around, his face was different. His mouth contorted and his eyes changed. The red hue returned. He looked at me as a predator looked at its prey. He must have seen the startled look on my face at his change because he smiled menacingly. A smile that showed two incredibly long canine teeth protruding from the top of his mouth.

I looked to my left and then to my right at Leather Jacket and Baldy. Their smiles also showed off their canines. Fangs ready to pierce and rip through flesh.

Silas stepped closer, his mouth open and teeth in full display. His eyes burned a deep red.

Suddenly, a flash of images popped into my head. I was thrust into the past, into my past, but not from any time that I could remember.

"Mike, come on," Martin yelled.

"Martin, where are you?" ten-year-old me yelled back. "Marty, I'm scared. It's dark, and I don't like it here."

Red eyes burned in the darkness up ahead. I heard a commotion in front of me and Martin's scream for help. I ran to him, to the only light I could see. Those red eyes in the pitch-dark tunnel.

I couldn't breathe and started coughing. The coughing brought me out of my memory trance. A memory I didn't have in my Ultranet; a memory vault that was permanent. Where did that come from?

My arms dropped to my side. Realization of the present came rushing back to me. The alley filled with a thick smoke. A canister spun in circles on the ground. Smoke erupted from it. My captors were coughing, grabbing their throats.

I glanced to my right. Baldy stood upright, clawing at his throat, leaving scratch marks. The fog grew thicker, and I could no longer see the end of the building or the parking lot beyond it. A silver chain wrapped around Baldy's neck like a whip, and he was gone.

Silas flailed his arms around and hit me in the chest, driving me back into the wall. My head slammed into the cinder block for the second time that night. Silas grabbed Leather Jacket and disappeared.

I collapsed as my vision blurred again. A ringing sound in my ears drowned out any noise. I struggled to maintain consciousness; a battle I was quickly losing. I turned to my right and thought I saw Baldy on the ground. I blinked to bring my eyes back in focus. Baldy wasn't next to me, after all, at least not all of him. His severed head rocked a foot from me.

In a panic, I tried to escape. My vision darkened as I moved. I made it a few feet before collapsing onto my side. I fought to keep my eyes open. My vision went in and out. I strained to see anything in the thick smoke.

Out of the shadow, two figures walked toward me. I tried to raise up on my arms but fell back down. The two figures approached and were close enough for me to make out who they were—John and Jane.

Great. From someone or something that tried to kill me to my stalkers. Jane rolled up a silver chain as she bent down close to me.

"You," I said as I lost my battle with consciousness.

15

My head hurt. I tried to open my eyes and the pain rushed in deeper. I rolled over in bed, trying to find the one comfortable spot that would take all the pain away. My pillow felt thin and flat, barely existent on my aching head.

What did I drink last night? I reached for Brittany to tell her about the horrible nightmare I had. A skeleton with blonde hair had her neck sliced by some maniac who then transformed into a vampire. He had two friends who held me down but one of them lost his head…literally.

My arm fell off the side of the bed and hit the concrete floor. Our bed is not that low to the ground. I brought my arm underneath the bed and felt the frame. I wasn't on my bed but a cot. Where the hell was I?

I opened my eyes, powering past the screams in my head. The events of the previous night rushed back to me. It was a nightmare, and unfortunately not a dream. The cot creaked loudly as I sat upright and swung my legs over the side. My head swam, and I almost fell back down. I steadied myself and observed my surroundings.

I was in a storage area, but the walls were shelving lined with supplies such as jugs of cleaners, bleach, and lighter fluid. The cot sat in the middle of the make-shift room. More shelves stretched out forming almost a hallway. The ceiling reached high above with rafters at the top. This was a warehouse.

A soft mumble of voices emanated from close by. I sat motionless for a minute, listening. I made out Jane's Australian accent and John's baritone. Random words mixed in with laughter.

I planted my feet firmly on the ground and rose off the cot. My head filled with excruciating pain. I slowly walked down the hallway, trying to navigate my way out. A pipe lay on a shelf to my right. I grabbed it and held it in front of me.

The closer I got to the voices, the more I could make out. They were talking about what happened last night. Silas had escaped. I crept further down the hallway, closer to the voices. I didn't want to go to them, but it seemed that was the way my path was taking me.

"Love, stop goofing off and come have a chat," Jane yelled.

I stopped and froze, raising the pipe to my shoulder, ready to attack, but secretly hoping she wasn't talking to me.

"Sergeant White," another voice said. "We'd love to make your acquaintance. We are here to help. You won't be needing the weapon."

I kept the pipe raised, ready to swing. The hallway opened into a conference room made out of fencing. A large table sat in the middle of the room surrounded by chairs. The fenced walls of the room had monitors suspended just above eye level. Computer desks lined the walls like cubicles in an office space. A few of the monitor screens had surveillance camera footage on them. One small window showed my cot. They saw me the whole time.

Five people occupied the workspace. I recognized John and Jane immediately. Jane sat on top of the table with one leg draped off the side. Two other men sat in the chairs around it. John stood on the opposite side. The last person sat in a chair next to a workstation, typing on the computer.

"Sergeant White," one of the men sitting said. He stood and walked to me. He was tall, standing just over six feet, and built like a football linebacker. He had broad shoulders, a square jawline, and a shaved bald head. I noticed a few shaving nicks. "Niki was telling me you have had quite the night."

"Niki?" I asked, confused and trying to orient myself.

"I'm John Sanchez," he continued. He held his hand out. "You can call me Jax."

I lowered the pipe, but still kept a good grip on it. I raised my hand and shook his. "Where am I?" I asked.

"A warehouse on the industrial side of town. Actually, not too far from where you work. Most people think it's abandoned and, for the most part, it is." Jax led me over to the table. "This is our current headquarters. Once our work is finished, we'll pack up shop and move on to the next place."

"What work?"

"We'll get to that. First things first. Welcome to the Night Crew," Jax said.

"That's what Boss likes to call us. Told him Suicide Squad would be better, but that was already taken," Jane—well Niki—said.

"Don't listen to her. She's always bitter."

"Niki Davis," she said, while hopping off the table. She extended her hand to me, and we shook. She wore a belt around her waist with a gun holster, a large knife, and the silver whip. She looked like a skinnier Lara Croft. She turned to Jax, "I'll give the introductions."

"Have at it," Jax said and stepped aside.

"Well, you've met the boss man. We try not to let him talk much. He can be very intense. Another person you probably recognize is standing over there," she pointed to John across the table. "This hunk of gorgeous man is Nathan Edwards, but only I can call him Nathan. He prefers Nate. And don't get any funny ideas. He's all mine."

Nate leaned over the table and shook my hand. "Pleasure," we both said.

"At the computer over there is Mr. Josh Campbell," Niki continued. "He's the technology guru and all-around geek. Most of what you see in here he built."

"Pardon me if I don't stand," Josh said and pointed at the wheelchair. I walked to Josh and shook his hand.

"And finally we have Scott Simmons in the other chair," Niki finished. "Scott is our jack of all trades. Need a bomb set, that's Scott. Car fixed. Scott. Lunch. Scott."

Bomb set?

"Nice to meet you," Scott said as he rose and shook my hand.

Jax stepped back into the conversation. "Is Thomas still out?" he asked Niki.

"I didn't see him come back this morning," she answered.

"He knows what he's doing. He's been around a lot longer than us."

I spoke up, "I appreciate the meet and greet, but I'm still in the dark. I'd like some fucking answers. What the fuck happened last night? And why have you two been following me?"

"Nate and I were trying to make sure you didn't do anything stupid. You know, like you ended up doing anyhow last night. Are you asking to become lunch meat?"

"Lunch meat? What are you even talking about?" I asked her. I needed answers and started to take offense at her implications. I felt a visit to Camp Anger coming soon.

"Yes, lunch meat. Silas alone would've drained you. Going against three of them by yourself, though," she shook her head at me, "you'd have been torn to pieces."

"Please stop talking in riddles. I was thrown into a wall. Twice. My head is pounding. Everything is fuzzy, and what I remember doesn't make any sense."

Niki turned to Jax. He nodded at her silent question.

"Alright, you asked for it. You'll probably want to sit down. It's time to step into The Twilight Zone," she said. "I mean that. In more ways than one, actually, although the movies sucked."

I grabbed a chair at the table, placing the pipe in front of me. Niki took a seat on the other side. Nate and Jax joined us at the table, while Scott and Josh turned back to their computers.

"This is going to sound like a lot of horse shit. It did to me when I first learned the truth, but you need to believe me. Try to keep an open mind," she said.

"I've seen a lot of shit. The way people can treat other people...well, try me. I doubt yours equals mine," or so I thought.

"Tragically, this is a whole new level of fucked up," she said and paused. She took a deep breath and continued.

"Do you believe in vampires?"

I sat there in silence for a minute. What the actual fuck did she just say! My gaze shifted from Jax to Nate and back to Niki. None of their facial expressions had changed.

"I'm waiting for the punchline. Vampire? Like Bram Stoker, Bela Lugosi, dark cape, 'I vaunt to suck your blood' vampire?"

"Well, they don't go around saying that, but yes, love, that."

Either this was the best deadpan comedy routine ever, or they all really believed this nonsense. Still, no one's facial expression had changed. "Are you telling me my wife was killed by a vampire? Creature of the night who turns into a bat, and you drive a stake through their heart?"

Jax leaned forward in his chair. "Yep, except the vampire who killed your wife is not a normal vampire. Silas is an Alpha. He's older, stronger, and has a following of Betas. You're lucky to be alive."

"I can't believe you all can keep straight faces."

"There are signs all over when a powerful Alpha is around," Jax said.

"Signs?"

"Did you notice the number of funerals happening when you buried your wife? How many missing children posters have you seen? Those are all signs. Vampires bring death. When it's bad enough, even the weather changes, as if the air itself is dying."

"You are insane. Vampires are merely a misunderstanding of some other as yet unidentified disease of the time."

Scott turned around in his chair. "I thought the same thing. Yet," he paused a moment, "vampire lore goes back thousands of years. There are occurrences all over the globe. Cultures spanned oceans, never interacted with one another, and still had similar legends."

"Look at the brains on Scott," Niki joked. "Told you, he's a jack of all trades. He knows a little about a lot. But he doesn't know shit about anything."

I leaned back in my chair and shook my head. Unbelievable. Why were they trying to convince me that a fictional character killed my wife?

I closed my eyes, and the images of Silas in my house and outside of the club popped back in. The fiery red eyes. Blood covering his pale face. If there ever was a caricature of a vampire, though, he fit it.

"You should have told him after Thomas got here," Nate told Jax and Niki. "Thomas would make a believer of him."

"Why is that?" I asked.

"Because," Niki answered, "Thomas is a bloody vampire himself. He is one of the few who happen to be on the side of the good guys."

"You have vampires who work for you?" I questioned, astonished. "Is there a kennel in the back with a werewolf, too?"

"Don't be silly," Niki answered. "Werewolves would tear a kennel to shreds."

There was a brief moment of silence. "Holy shit, you're serious. How many of you are there?" I looked around at all the gear. "And where do you get all of this funding?"

"We have friends in high places," Niki responded. "They keep our bank accounts full, and we try to take care of the infestation on the streets. The travel is nice. We've been hunting Silas for a long time, and this is the closest we've ever been."

"We did have a seven-person crew, but we lost someone a few weeks back. It hurts but it happens," Jax said taking over the conversation. The whole table's demeanor shrunk at the somberness of his tone. "Everyone here knows the cost and the reward for what we do. It's what it means to be part of the Night Crew." They each slowly nodded as he spoke. "I want to grow us to seven again. You have a score to settle, and one hell of an impressive service record."

I took a moment to process what he just said. "You want me to be a part of this lunacy?" The memory of me holding Brit as she died in my arms came back. I promised her I would make this right. Promised her I'd find him. "Yes, I want revenge."

"Then join us and do that," Niki interrupted. "Help us kill him."

"This is a lot. I need some time to think about it," I said. "Can one of you take me back to my hotel? I'd love to take something for my head and hope I don't have brain damage from hitting the wall."

"Twice," Josh chimed in while holding up two fingers, still facing his computer screen.

"Yes," I agreed. "Twice."

"I got you," Jax said.

"His scent!" Josh hollered.

"My scent?"

He spun his wheelchair around and slid up to the table. "Yeah. When an Alpha like Silas gets your scent, they'll track you down. We'll need to mask you."

"Mask me? How?" I asked.

Josh rolled over to me. He held up a syringe gun. "This is a shot of pure garlic extract. It's perfectly safe and won't hurt a bit. Granted, if you sweat, you'll smell like an Italian restaurant, but it'll mask your scent from Silas. You'll be harder to find."

I leaned toward Josh, and he placed the gun against my neck. As he pulled the trigger, I felt the sting of the needle. The extract burned going in. He'd conveniently skipped that bit of information. I rubbed at the injection site to help the serum dissipate.

"Am I safe to leave now?" I asked, frustrated.

Jax stood up. "Follow me."

Nate and Niki also stood up from their chairs. She held out her hand to me. "See you soon," she said confidently as we shook. She turned and threw her arms around Nate. "Take me to bed, beautiful."

I followed Jax to the front door of the warehouse. Night Crew headquarters. We passed an armory of supplies: knives, guns, smoke canisters. Two SUV's were parked inside as well. They had tow gear on the back, and lights mounted to the roof. A winch was secured to the front.

He opened the front door, and I winced at the bright light of morning.

16

For the first time since staying at the hotel, I found it uncomfortable. I paced the small room, unable to stop myself from moving. I walked from the door, past the bathroom on my right, past the television on my left and bed on my right, to the window, and then back to the door. Occasionally, I pulled the curtain back to glance out of the window. There was one point of entry, but it was also my only escape route. It was too high up to jump out of the window and survive. Could vampires jump out of my window and be fine? Could they jump up to my window? Can vampires turn into bats and fly up to me?

More importantly, was I truly having these thoughts? Actually contemplating if vampires could reach a third story window? Vampires. Blood sucking creatures of the night.

As quickly as possible, I ran to the bathroom and dry heaved into the toilet. I collapsed onto the linoleum floor between the shower stall and the toilet. My hands felt the coldness of the floor. I flushed the toilet, then placed my throbbing head on the cold porcelain.

Closing my eyes, I brought back up the night of Brittany's murder. With my new perspective, I rewatched the events. My imagination filled in what probably happened before I arrived. I couldn't imagine the terror she must've felt. The fear in her eyes as that monster tore into her. A real, live, actual monster ripping away the flesh of her neck and gorging on her lifeblood as her heart continued to beat. Her heart betraying her, killing her as it fought to keep her alive.

With my head still pressed against the cold porcelain, I cried.

I wasn't sure how long I stayed like that. It felt like hours before I finally pulled myself off the floor, wiping the tears and snot from my face. I popped two Motrin finally and dropped myself onto the bed. I crooked my forearm over my forehead and stared up at the ceiling.

My wife was killed by a vampire. A group of mercenaries calling themselves the Night Crew traveled the globe hunting and killing vampires. And they wanted me to join them. I thought through the ramifications of such a decision, starting with the pros: I get revenge on Silas for killing Brittany, and travel the world as a vampire hunter. Con: I could be killed. But then I would be with Brittany again. I still get my vengeance, though. I kept coming back to that reason alone. Either I can enact my vengeance and live up to the promise I made Brittany as she lay dying in my arms, or I can sit here in my own misery, knowing I had the opportunity to act and didn't.

You know the answer, Brit said as I stared at the ceiling. *You know what you need to do.*

I closed my eyes and pictured myself lying on our bed. Brittany lay next to me on her side. Her white nightgown flowed down the length of her torso and ended halfway down her thigh. The strap on one shoulder continuously slipped off, but she didn't care. She knew it teased the hell out of me.

"I really miss you," I told her. I kept my eyes closed tightly, not wanting to slip out of the memory.

"I know you do," she said. "One day, we'll be together again. But until then, you have work to do. They could use your help. You can stop what happened to me from happening to anyone else."

"I wish I didn't work late that night. I should've been home with you."

"Then we'd both be buried in the cemetery, right now," she said.

"But we'd be together," I responded.

"We will be again. But first, help them save lives."

I knew she was right. She always was. Her hair draped across the pillow while she propped herself up on one arm. She leaned into me. With my eyes closed, I felt her gentle lips kiss the side of my cheek. I held on to that sensation, the slight tingle of electricity, the nerve endings that fired from memory, before feeling the emptiness of the bed next to me.

She was gone.

I lay there a moment longer before slowly opening my eyes. The empty ceiling stared back down at me.

Three loud knocks thundered against the door to the hotel room, startling me out of bed. I shuffled over and looked through the peep hole in the door. Detective Jennings stood in the hallway waiting for me to open the door.

"Mike," he shouted. "Are you awake?" He hammered on the door three more times.

I unlatched the lock and opened the door.

"You look like shit," he told me as he walked into my hotel room.

"Having your wife murdered will do that to you," I snapped back. I turned around and followed him in.

Jennings slowly walked past the bed, pausing for a minute to pick up the bottle of Motrin on the dresser. He shook it, listening to the last remaining pills rattling around, and sat it back down. He walked to the window and pointed to the couch.

"Sure, go ahead," I said, and he took a seat. "You could've just called to give me an update. You don't have to give me the personal treatment."

"Perfectly fine. Let's say I was in the neighborhood," he said. "So, when are you heading back to your place?"

"I'm hoping to soon," I lied. "It was hard walking through it the other day. Are your forensic guys all done?"

"Yeah, they're pretty quick at what they do," he answered. He crossed his legs and rested his arms across my jacket resting on the back of the couch.

Make yourself at home.

"Glad to hear you will be heading back there. Good to start moving forward again. You stay here and wallow in depression for too long...well, that's when people do dumb things."

"I bet. So, do you have an update? Find the guy who killed Brittany?"

"Your one-armed man? Nope. Besides your wife's, forensics only found your DNA there, but that's to be expected, right?"

He was fishing. He didn't have a clue what he was dealing with.

"Guess he wasn't there long enough to leave any," I said. "You came all the way here to tell me you didn't have any new information? Sounds like a waste of taxpayer dollars, Detective."

"What have you been doing since the last time we spoke?" he asked.

"You mean since you accused me of killing my wife at her graveside with her not even in the ground yet?"

"Yeah, let's go with that," he said smugly.

"Just trying to survive," I said equally smug.

"Have you been doing any of your own detective work? Some husbands, when they don't feel like the police are doing enough, decide they can do the police work better. With all the movies and of course your impressive service record, I don't want you to do something stupid and end up in trouble."

That was twice in only a few hours someone cautioned me about doing something stupid. "Detective, I'm just hoping you bring me promising news soon while trying to put my life back together."

He stood from the couch. "Good to hear, Mike. Good to hear. Let's just make sure you keep to that and leave the police work to the professionals." He headed toward the door, stopping at the pill bottle again. "Don't do too many of those. Can give you ulcers."

I beat him to the door and opened it for him. As he stepped into the hallway, I said, "Thanks for the advice. And Detective, next time, just call." I quickly closed the door and latched it.

Moments later, my back was on the bed with the crappy hotel pillow bundled into a ball beneath my head. I fell asleep within minutes of Detective John leaving.

My phone rang. I grabbed it from the nightstand. Unknown number.

"Hello?" I questioned.

"Mike," Jax began.

I fully opened my eyes. Hardly any light streamed in from the curtain crack of the window. I glanced at the clock. Seventeen hundred hours. I'd been asleep for almost seven hours.

"No patience?" I asked him.

"We have a location," Jax said ignoring my question.

"A location?" I asked, my interest piqued.

"Definitely a den. Been confirmed that Silas has been there. I know you haven't made up your mind yet, but we'd love for you to tag along. Give you a chance to see what it's all about."

"I'm in." The moment he said Silas could be there, I was sold. "I'll grab my coat."

"Five minutes."

17

"What'd you expect?" Scott asked as he pulled into the subdivision. Ahead of us, Nate drove the SUV with Niki and Jax.

The neighborhood looked like typical suburbia. Trash cans sat on the curb waiting for tomorrow's garbage truck to pick them up. Kids' bicycles propped against houses or laid in the yard. It was the kind of neighborhood where they trusted it would still be there in the morning. I bet some of the cars were unlocked as well.

The houses varied between one and two stories. Each had the same general look. It was obvious the same contracting company built all the houses in the neighborhood. Every few houses I had deja vu - the same architecture, the same color scheme.

"I'm not sure what I was expecting, but it wasn't this," I told him.

"My first raid, I thought I'd see Dracula's castle or a cave, like in *Lost Boys*. I was shocked to learn how close a den of vampires could live to you, and you'd never know. It's even easier today. How many people actually know their neighbors? Even in a nice, Norman Rockwell neighborhood like this? Families come and go. People buy these houses and rent them out. Some people might know the person next door, but not two houses down."

He was right. Brittany and I knew a handful of people on our street, but not everyone. Next door neighbors and across the street maybe, but I'd never spoken to the people more than two houses down.

Nate turned the corner onto the next street and stopped in front of a two-story house. Scott pulled up behind him as everyone started to pile out.

"Shouldn't we be doing this during the day?" I asked. I gazed at the evening sky which was quickly turning to dusk.

"Night's better," Niki said.

"During the day, don't vampires burst into flames or something because of the sun?"

"Don't believe the movies," Jax said. "At night, vampires are more lethal, so they have a tendency to stick around and fight it out. During the day, though, they aren't as predictable. I'll take predictable every time. Keeps us alive."

Scott and Nate opened the back of the SUVs and started pulling out gear. I took the opportunity to examine the house. The grass mowed, the driveway recently swept, and Halloween decorations in the front windows. I found it hard to believe a house full of vampires would set out pumpkins on the front porch and have corny, vampire window clings attached to the front windows. The house had a two-car garage door on our right.

"You're sure vampires live here?" I asked. I couldn't wrap my head around what I was seeing.

"Yes," Jax said. "Thomas has been here for the past three days now. This is a den. Time to gear up."

Nate handed me a 9mm pistol, a machete, and an earpiece. Niki caught the machete Scott tossed her way with one hand and her silver chain with the other. Obviously, they'd done this routine multiple times before. Jax passed Nate a pump action shotgun.

"Two-minute drill," Jax said. "Comms on?"

"Wait," I said. "I'm behind the curve here. My only references to vampires are the movies. What's the plan? How do you kill these things?"

"Short version," Nate said. "Take off their head."

Jax chimed in. "We'll cover all the nuances of vampire hunting later. Call this Trial by Fire. We wanted to hit this den as quickly as possible since we had Intel. But, like Nate said, take off their heads. Worry about the bodies later."

"Why a two-minute drill?" I asked.

"Police response time," Niki said. "As soon as someone calls 9-1-1, we've only got a few minutes to clean up the scene. Last thing we want is a police chase through the city."

Then, Josh's voice blared in my head. "How's the sound? Are we ready for business?"

"We hear you," Jax said. "Assignments. Nate, you're with me. We'll take the back and sweep the downstairs. Scott and Niki, front door and head upstairs."

"Who am I going with?" I asked. I shifted back and forth on my feet, adrenaline coursing through my veins. I had to willfully suppress memories of my first tour in Afghanistan. So many of those same worries and anxieties welled up inside of me. What's waiting just beyond the door? Over there, we had a good idea what was on the other side. But here? According to this group of people, vampires, actual vampires, lived in the house we stood in front of. Monsters, to possibly include the one Silas who killed Brit, waited for us, and these people calmly acted like this was a normal day.

A part of me still wondered if this was happening. Were there vampires, and the Night Crew hunted them? Or were they some kill squad taking out a nice family in the suburbs?

"Stay here. If we get a runner, they're all yours."

"Stay here? Alone?"

If monsters existed, alone was the last place I wanted to be.

"You'll be fine," Jax said, clapping me on the shoulder. "Based on the intel, this one's small. Should have it cleared and cleaned in no time. And with all your special forces training, you won't have anything to worry about."

I took a few long breaths and steadied my nerves. I thought about what Nate said. Just take off their heads. That didn't sound disturbing at all, but what the hell. I only had to worry if there was a runner.

"I'm good catching any runners," I said, not wanting to sound terrified. "When I get the rules learned, I'd like an upgrade, though."

"Love the enthusiasm, Mike," Jax responded with a smile. He turned to the group as we stood on the street in front of the house. "I know I don't need to tell you but watch yourselves in there. They're fast, and they're strong. Although Thomas confirmed Silas has been here, I doubt he is now. Be prepared if he is, though. Do not try to take him down alone. You will lose. Be smart and take care of business. Hands in." Everyone put a hand in a circle. I followed suit and slid mine in. "Lord, protect us from evil as we deliver Your judgment to them. Amen."

"Amen," everyone said in unison. Scott and Nate crossed themselves.

"Josh, two minutes. Keep your ears open for 9-1-1. Positions."

The group dispersed. Nate and Jax split to the back fence. Scott and Niki approached the front door. I stood on the sidewalk by the cars. We waited silently for Nate and Jax to be in position. I nearly jumped out of my skin when I heard the gate being driven closed by the wind.

The street was empty. A steady breeze blew past the houses. I heard the scraping of leaves across the asphalt. The unusually cold air sank into me.

My heart pounded in my chest as I anxiously waited for something, anything to happen.

It felt like hours until Jax finally said, "Go on three."

"Boss, bad news," Josh interrupted. "Suspicious activity call. Clock starting. Two minutes."

"Three, two, one. Go!"

I saw Scott and Niki break into the front door. Through the windows, I saw Nate and Jax enter through the back door. I stood alone, their voices in my head.

Scott: "Taking stairs."

Jax: "Living room clear."

I heard doors opening and quick breathing.

Jax: "Master bedroom clear."

A fridge door opened.

Nate: "Confirm vamp den. Fridge is full of blood jugs and bags."

"Blood jugs and bags?" I asked, not meaning to out loud.

Nate: "For that midday snack."

Josh: "Minute forty-five remaining."

Scott: "Five bedrooms upstairs. First clear."

A flash appeared in an upstairs window and then a loud gunshot broke the silence. It left a ringing in my ear.

Niki: "Three biters."

Scott: "Right behind you, Niki."

Another gunshot clacked through the air. A blood-curdling scream echoed through the earpiece, accompanied by what sounded like a cleaver hitting a slab of meat. In my head, I could imagine what Niki's machete was doing. I remembered the head of last night's attacker lying next to me.

Josh: "Another call for shots fired. Minute fifteen."

Niki: "Clear."

Jax: "Downstairs clear. Checking garage."

Scott: "Next bedroom clear."

Josh: "One minute left. Officer en route."

Jax: "Four in garage. They're barricaded in. Nate, hurry."

Through the windows and the open front door, I saw Nate go down the hall and turn toward the garage door. I heard a thud as he collided with the door, forcing it open.

Jax: "Silver in."

I heard the familiar sound of a flash grenade go off, followed by the same silvery gray mist I'd seen the night before.

Josh: "Forty-five seconds."

The wind carried an ever-growing sound of police sirens.

Multiple people coughed inside the garage. I heard two gunshots followed by the sound of metal hitting flesh. In my mind's eye, I saw heads rolling.

Nate: "Garage clear."

Josh: "Thirty seconds."

Niki: "Last room. Shit! Mike, one just hurdled us. Coming your way."

I held the 9mm in my hand and took aim at the open front door. His feet bound down the stairs lightning quick, and in an instant, he stood on the front porch staring at me.

When I saw his face, my Ultranet fired off. Pictures streamed into my head. I'd seen his face before, but where? Suddenly, I was thrust back to the day I buried Brittany. I made my way to the hotel after buying Motrin and passed a missing person's flyer. The young kid, David, was twelve and had been missing for a week. I remembered the dirty blond hair and green eyes as he posed for what was probably his most recent, and now last, school photo.

I came out of my Ultranet and stared straight ahead at the twelve-year-old from the flyer. The 9mm dropped just slightly.

David must've noticed. He opened his mouth in a wide smile, revealing sharp fangs protruding from his upper and lower jawline. From the front porch, he lunged at me, clearing the distance with unbelievable speed, driving his shoulder into me.

The collision drove me to the ground. The 9mm shot across the yard. All I had now was the machete that rested in the sheath on my hip. I tried to reach for it, but I had just enough time to raise my arms before he was on top of me. His powerful hands pushed my shoulders to the ground as his head drew closer to my throat. He snapped with his teeth, trying to reach far enough forward to bury them in my neck. My forearms pushed back against his throat. It was the only thing keeping him from biting my head off. My other hand tried for the machete but couldn't free it from the sheath.

I could feel his hands crushing into my shoulders. I was going to die in this front yard by a twelve-year-old vampire. Vampire! Because somehow vampires were real. My arm was losing the battle, and his face grew closer and closer to my throat.

I heard voices in my ear but couldn't make anything out. My blood pulsated unbearably loud. The voices of the Night Crew sounded like I heard them through water. Just past David's head, I saw Jax and Niki come out of the front door. They stood there watching. Why the hell were they just standing there and not coming to help me? I had a brief moment believing they were going to watch me die. New guy couldn't cut it.

My eyes focused back on David's face, fangs that drew dangerously close. Another image flashed in my head that I didn't recognize. The second time it had happened in as many days. I stood in a dark tunnel. My childhood friend, Martin, cried up ahead of me. His cry turned into a low sob and drifted into nothing. In the darkness, I saw red, burning eyes staring at me. Two blood drenched incisors moved closer to me.

Now was not the time, brain!

Suddenly two hands clamped down on the side of David's head, snapping me back into the present. His head spun around unnaturally fast. I heard the sound of his neck breaking in multiple places as he no longer stared at me but up at the sky. The force on my shoulders let up.

A man stood on top of David, holding David's head. He had jet black hair and wore a long, thin, black trench coat. His face had familiar features I couldn't quite pin down. He placed a foot on top of David's back and pressed down. At the same time, he drove his arms up. I heard David's neck rip apart as his head detached from his body. Veins and muscle sinews, plus a few vertebrae remained attached to the head. David's body fell forward, and his neck landed on my stomach, covering me in blood as it drained from his body.

I peered up at the man still holding David's head and realized he was a vampire. He tossed the head next to me and started to reach down. I quickly scrambled backward in a crab walk and reached the 9mm on the ground. I grabbed it and swung it around, ready to fire. Before I could, though, Jax and Niki stood next to the vampire. "Woah, Mike. Stop, stop!" Niki yelled. "Meet Thomas Price."

Thomas turned to Jax. "This is the new guy?" he asked in a very unimpressed tone. He even had one skeptical eyebrow raised.

"Haven't had time to train him yet," Jax responded.

I dropped onto my back, my heart still racing. I laid my arms on the ground above my head and sat the pistol down.

Thomas offered me his hand. I took it, and he pulled me to my feet with ease.

"Next time, don't hesitate," he said, turning back to Jax.

"Hey guys," Josh said. "Bought you some additional time by rerouting the dispatched address. Dispatch is going to fix it as soon as they realize. Clean up and get out of there."

"Grab a body," Jax said.

"What?" I asked. I heard the order, but still had trouble processing it.

"Do what Nate and Scott are doing," he responded, knowing there wasn't time to explain.

I glanced over at Nate. He had a body over his shoulder and a head in his hands. He tossed both into the back of the SUV. Scott followed close behind him doing the same thing

"Grab the blood from the fridge and the empty grenade canisters," Scott said. "The place needs to look empty."

I hurried inside and emptied the contents of the refrigerator, carrying an armload of blood bags back to the SUV. After dropping my cargo into the back, I rushed back inside. The only canister was in the garage. I grabbed it and headed back out.

"All clean?" Jax asked, jogging to his SUV.

"All clean," I answered and returned to the seat I rode here in.

Between the two SUV's, we had eight heads, eight headless bodies, and dozens of blood bags. Scott and Jax started up the cars and peeled out. We turned the corner, just as I saw police lights turn onto the road from the opposite end.

"Next time," Josh dropped into our ears. "Let's not cut it so close. See you guys back at HQ."

18

Scott backed our SUV into the garage door and parked in front of the other one. All three of us, Scott, Thomas, and I, hopped out, and Scott walked around to the back. I followed. He opened the back gate; the bodies and heads casually stacked inside.

Josh came up behind us in his wheelchair. "Incinerator is fired up and ready," he said.

"Thanks," Scott responded. "Mike, roll me that cart over there." He pointed over by the wall. It looked like it would be perfect for industrial laundry use.

I went over to the cart, grabbed it, and pushed it over to our SUV. Scott grabbed the first body and tossed it into the cart. Figuring out what we were doing, I joined in. Headless bodies and bodiless heads filled the cart. Streaks of blood stained the cloth as we dropped vampire remains into it.

Glancing at the other car, I noticed we were the only two around. "Just us?" I asked.

"Nate and Niki were on toasting last time. Our turn."

"Toasting?"

Scott wiped the sweat from his forehead. Outside, the air still had a chill in it, especially when the wind blew. Inside, though, it was really warm.

"We bring everything back and throw it in the incinerator. Can you imagine the news reports if the authorities found a house full of decapitations? And then if they started doing autopsies or medical studies on vampire bodies? Part of why we do this is so the public doesn't have to find out about the things that go bump in the night. It's why clean-up is so important. Imagine the headlines, Buckets of Blood and Headless Corpses in Suburbia. That would draw some attention.

"This cart is full. Push it and follow me."

Scott led the way to the back corner of the building. I could see the glow of the computer screens as we passed the room I was in yesterday. The room where they sat me down and told me my wife had been killed by an alpha vampire named Silas. Two days ago, I had no idea vampires existed. Now I pushed a cart full of dead ones to an incinerator to destroy their remains. What a difference a day makes.

The incinerator sat in the back corner. It had a huge smokestack that went up the side of the warehouse and out the top. There was a glass front with red flames dancing inside of it. The heat radiated as we moved closer to it. Scott grabbed a large oven mitt and opened the glass door. It felt like every hair on my face would burn off as the heat wave hit me. He pulled a large conveyor belt out of the front. It looked like a huge metal table sitting in front of the fire.

Scott started unloading the cart, reaching for a body and tossing it onto the belt. He flipped a switch, and it started rolling to the flames. I added a head and another body and then it rolled into the fire. After the first two went in, he clenched a huge metal rod and shoved it into the incinerator. The bodies crumbled apart, making room for more.

"How long have you been doing this?" I asked him after we finished unloading the cart and headed back for the second load.

"I've been a part of the Night Crew for about five years," he said.

"Guessing you've seen a lot over the past five years?"

He gave a brief chuckle. "You have no idea. The world is getting crazier every day. When I joined up, we maybe found a nest like today's once every month. And when we did, that would be the only one in the city. But now, we know Silas is growing his numbers. We know there are more than the one we just cleared. He's still here and hasn't run."

"That's unusual?" I asked.

"Very. Jax has been chasing Silas for at least ten years, and Thomas has been for much longer. Typically, as they get close, Silas knows it, and he takes off. He establishes a nest, and we clear it out, but... he is usually out of town long before we get there. Something's changed. He's quickly building an army."

We loaded up the remaining bodies from the two SUVs and went back to the incinerator. Walking to it was what I could only imagine a trip into Hell would feel like. The heat intensified with each step. This time it felt hotter, as if the dead vampires from the first load had created a raging inferno inside. Scott led the way again, and I pushed.

"How did you get dragged into all of this?" I asked.

My mouth was dry as if all the moisture in my body had been evaporated. I tried to lick my chapped lips, but my tongue was sandpaper rubbing over jagged rocks. The heat pouring out of the incinerator was unbearable.

"Lose someone like I did?" I finally spat out.

He held up his hand with one finger, and I interpreted that as he'd tell me in a minute. It made me feel better to know that obviously he was feeling a little parched as well.

We tossed the last of the vampire remains on the belt, and he used the rod to shove them in. Using the rod, he closed the glass door. I could still feel the heat emanating from the incinerator, but the direct inferno-like wave subsided.

Scott stared at his watch for one minute, then stepped to the side of the incinerator and hit the kill switch. The fire slowly died away as it lost fuel inside the cavern. The orange glow withered, leaving only darkness inside.

"Want some water?" he asked.

"Please," I choked out.

Scott nodded and said, "Push the cart back where you found it."

I obliged and took the blood-stained cart back to the front of the warehouse. I went out to the vehicles and the fence when Scott met me with a bottle of water. I unscrewed the top and gulped down two thirds of it. The coolness of the water felt like Heaven after breathing in scorched air.

"You asked if I lost someone," he said as we trudged past the SUVs and supplies, toward the conference area where the others sat. "I didn't lose anyone before joining up with Night Crew. I was fortunate in that regard. Most were recruited like you were, had a special set of skills and lost a loved one. I stumbled upon the Night Crew my last year of grad school."

"Grad school?" I asked.

"Senior year. MIT. Engineering. Jax posted an ad."

"Wait, he posted an ad looking for a vampire hunter?" I asked in disbelief.

"Not exactly," he laughed. "You know the mist grenades we use? I think Nate said they threw one when they rescued you from Silas, and I heard him yell silver this evening. I built those.

"His ad was for a special canister release mechanism. Aerial dispersal of silver nitrate.

"It doesn't affect us, but the silver weakens a vampire. It sticks to their lungs, and they usually can't breathe, going into a coughing fit. It gives us just enough of an opening to do what we need to do."

We turned the corner at a four-rack shelf, and the rest of the crew sat around the conference table. Niki leaned back in her chair with her feet on the table. Jax had a laptop and was typing away. Nate talked to Josh. I sat next to Thomas and glanced in his direction. He held a glass of thick, red liquid in his hand. He took a drink, savoring it.

"Please tell me that's a Merlot," I said.

Josh looked at me and then over at Thomas. He turned back to me, grinning. "That's not Merlot."

My stomach turned over. I held back the urge to throw up, but only barely. "That's..." I swallowed hard. "That's a glass of blood?"

Thomas took another sip as if he was a wine connoisseur. He could see my revulsion and played into it. "Freshly squeezed. From one of the bags you loaded up," he said. His cheeks, which were a pale white color, reddened as he drank. "I haven't fed in a week, and just like you, I have to stay nourished." He took another drink.

"That's so disgusting," I said.

"Every living thing does what it has to do to survive," he said. "Vampires thirst for blood to quench our hunger. It replenishes us. Heals our injuries. Restores us."

"I didn't think vampires were living things."

"You have a lot to learn about vampires. Speaking of... you almost got yourself killed. Never hesitate. A vampire is not a person, no matter the face you see. A vampire is an animal, a vile creature that shouldn't exist."

I stared at him as he spoke. It was obvious how he felt about vampires. He hated his own kind. I wanted to know how far his hatred for them extended.

"A creature that shouldn't exist? Present company excluded, I'm guessing."

"Do you think I want to be this way?" he snapped back. His eyes burned red. The other conversations around the table fell silent. I felt everyone's eyes on me.

"Do you think I asked to be this thing I am? I wasn't given a choice. This was thrust upon me." He turned to everyone else at the table. "I feel I must excuse myself," he said, standing with the cup in his hand. He disappeared around the corner, and a moment later, I heard the door slam shut.

"I didn't mean to upset him," I said.

"Thomas is very sensitive," Niki said. "We all owe him. He's saved each one of us at some point, including you on your first outing. It's hard to get through to him how important he is to us. Thomas has his own vendetta he is trying to free himself from."

"What do you mean?" I asked.

"The Night Crew hasn't always been around," she continued. "Vampires, especially young ones, have a really bad thirst. He hasn't told us many stories from before he learned to control the hunger, but the ones he has aren't good. The legends are worse. He hates himself for what he did, the lives he took. I think, in his head, he has a tally of how many he needs to save to make up for the ones he took."

"That is some rough shit," I said. "I knew guys in the military who struggled with what we had to do, but we had counseling services, others we could talk to."

"Thomas," Jax said, "has a lot of demons."

I sat in silence for a few minutes, letting the conversation fade away along with the rising emotions. I finally broke the silence.

"I want in."

"You want in?" Jax asked.

"Yes, I want in. I can't go back into the world without getting vengeance for what Silas did to Brit, and I can't do it alone. Teach me about vampires and how to be a hunter, so I can kill Silas. I'll be an asset to you along the way, but once he's dead, though, I'm going back to my life. I owe it to Brittany to push through and find normal again."

Closing my eyes, I could see her smiling next to me. She would want me to find peace and carry on. In the grief counseling where we met, that was something they taught us, and she held true to it. Move through the stages of grief. Get to Camp Acceptance. While Silas was still a threat, I could justify staying in Camp Anger, but afterward...

Jax sat there for a minute. He extended his hand over to me, and I took it. "Welcome to the Night Crew," he said. "Your training starts tomorrow. But tonight, drinks in honor of a good clearing. Josh, mind grabbing a bottle or two? Bourbon. The good stuff. Not the shit I water down and usually give you guys."

19

Brittany tied her long red hair into a ponytail, but she missed a few strands. The wind blew them into her face, and she kept pushing them out of the way. She looked stunning in her one-piece bathing suit. It enveloped her, hugging all the right spots.

"Mike," she hollered. "Aren't you going to join me?"

The bright sun made me squint despite wearing my sunglasses. I sat on the beach as she danced in the water in front of me. Every day I fell more and more in love with her.

Brittany fell backward into the water, floating there for a moment before raising back up. Her skin glistened with the ocean water rolling off it. How could someone like me be so lucky?

"Get off your butt and get out here. The water feels great."

"Can't I just enjoy the view?" I hollered back.

"Enjoying the view, huh?" she said. "How about now?" She slipped a strap off her shoulder.

I propped myself up a little more on the beach, watching her. "Looking great, beautiful."

"And now?" she said, letting the other strap of her bathing suit fall down her arm.

I glanced around the beach. Fortunately, no one stood close by to see my wife taunt me. "Definitely looks great. You better stop before someone sees you."

"Oh," she said. She seductively strolled toward me, the shoulder straps of her bathing suit dangling down her arms. She came closer. Since the straps no longer supported the top of her suit, the front of it slowly crept down with every step she took. She brought her shoulders together, exaggerating the cleavage that became increasingly more noticeable.

The water covered her ankles as she stood a few feet in front of me. I kept staring at her, not taking my eyes away. Suddenly, she kicked out with her feet, splashing me with ocean water.

"You little wench," I said. I jumped up from the beach and ran at her. I grabbed her around her waist, picked her up, and we both fell into the water laughing.

"Mike," a voice said as I kissed Brittany in the blue waters. "Mike, wake up."

I slowly opened my eyes, leaving the peace and serenity, and thrusting myself back into the present. Out of a memory and back into this harsh reality. A reality with no more trips to the beach, or seductive walks out of the water, or laughing as we fell into each other's arms. Those were only memories now. Memories I hoped to slip into as often as I could.

Jax stood over me. I sat up from the cot I'd slept in last night and rolled my neck. It and my back felt sore. The cot was not the most comfortable thing to sleep on. Pain killers would be my friend today.

"What time is it?" I asked.

"Zero eight hundred," he said. "Nate cooked breakfast. Eat. We have training to do. You have a lot to learn and not much time to learn it."

I placed my feet on the concrete floor and raised myself off the cot. I stretched everything out and followed Jax to the kitchen area. The smell of bacon cooking could have led me just as easily. The aroma filled the entire warehouse.

I covered my plate with eggs, toast, and bacon and sat at a small table. Jax sat across from me.

"I've seen a lot of movies about vampires," I said between bites. "There's a lot of differences between them. What's true?" Despite what I saw just yesterday, it was still hard to believe I was asking about what was real with vampires. All my life, vampires were just something in books and movies. Not something people lived next to or fought in a front yard.

"That's as good a place as any to start," Jax said. He leaned back in his chair. "Let me get the basics out of the way. First, sunlight doesn't kill vampires. That came from the old silent film, *Nosferatu*. They are weaker in the sunlight, and prefer to sleep during that time, but that's about it. No bursting into flames and, thank God, they don't sparkle."

"No sparkling," I quipped.

"Because they are weaker, it makes them less predictable like I said last night. Weaker doesn't mean they aren't strong as Hell... and fast. We came across a group of vampires in upstate New York that we tried to clean during the day. Five of them. My former team lead figured if they are weaker, they'd be easier to kill. A quick in and out. We killed two of them. Instead of sticking around to fight, the other three ran. I can still remember the screams as they sprinted into a crowd of people, blood spraying everywhere.

"To regain their strength, vampires need blood. You saw that with Thomas last night. Those three tried to drink while running from us; like they were Pac-man devouring power pellets, and we were the ghosts. We caught up with them, but not before ten people were slaughtered."

"At night, they think they have the upper hand, so they want to fight it out?"

Jax nodded. "They do have the upper hand. Always. Don't ever think you do. That kid was freshly turned and nearly took your head off. With age, they get stronger and have more powers. The more a vampire feeds, the stronger it gets. Alphas like Silas are the strongest we know of."

A thought occurred to me. "What causes them to lose their humanity? I mean, like you said, the kid was freshly turned. I saw a missing person poster for him just the other day. How did he go from, I'm assuming, a sweet, loving kid to trying to rip my throat apart?"

"The blood lust," Jax answered. "From what Thomas and others have said, and from what I've seen in those turned, it is all consuming. The thirst is so overpowering that there's no room for humanity. It's like gasping for air when you come up from being underwater too long. You do it out of survival, not because you want to. That kid had as much control over his hunger for blood as you do making your heart beat."

"But what about Thomas, Silas, and those who attacked me outside the night club?"

"Vampires gain control as they get older and stronger. Fledglings have no control."

"Fledglings?" I asked.

Jax smiled. "Freshly turned vampires. There is a ranking system among vampires. They start as a fledgling. As they get older and gain that strength and control, they move up in rank until eventually breaking away from their den and becoming an alpha."

"How many alphas are there?" I asked.

"Not many," Jax said while shrugging his shoulders. "Less than a dozen. They try to stake out a territory and stay in that area. Silas has been on the move. I think it's because of Thomas."

"Are we the only crew? Does anybody else have a vampire assisting them?"

Jax smiled. "No, there are other teams, and a few do contain vampires."

"How many other teams do this? Where does the funding come from? Who do you report to?" A million other questions came to mind along with those.

"Slow down," Jax said. "We'll get to all of that. For now, focus on learning about vampires. Now, where was I?"

"Silas is moving because of Thomas," I answered. "What makes him special?"

"Thomas is Silas's older brother," he said.

The memory of him standing over me holding David's head flooded back. His features seemed familiar at the time. I had searched my Ultranet and knew I'd never seen him before. That explained the familiarity. A family resemblance.

"Woah," I said, putting my fork down and sitting back in my chair.

"So we covered sunlight," Jax said, sending us back to our initial conversation. "Some of the other movie tropes. Vampires are allergic to silver. If enough silver gets in their system, it can kill them. If you want to torture a vampire, you do it with silver."

"Why would I want to torture a vampire and not just take their head off?"

"Same reason you would've tortured a terrorist. Information. If it would've been any other rogue Alpha's den, we would've interrogated one of them, but Silas doesn't give his fledglings any information. He's smarter than that.

"Back to silver. You've seen our silver grenades."

"Yeah, Scott told me he designed those for you."

"They've helped a lot. Probably what saved you from Silas the other night. The bullets we use have a silver covering on them. Completely silver bullets don't work well. They are lighter than lead so the accuracy sucks.

"Garlic is also a good deterrent. It doesn't hurt them or burn, but they will avoid the strong smell of garlic. It helps to hide things as well, like the shot Josh gave you to hide your scent."

"Are all of their senses heightened? Smell, sight, hearing?"

"The older the vampire, the more sensitive. Alphas are highly tuned with excellent sensing. Sneaking up on an Alpha is nearly impossible.

Fledglings are much easier. They are strong and their senses are better than ours, but it's nothing compared to Alphas."

"We cut off their heads last night. I thought to kill a vampire, you drove a wooden stake through its heart."

"For that to work, you have to precisely hit the heart. It doesn't have to be a wooden stake, either; you just need to damage the heart. But, since the heart is hard to get to, separating them from their head is simpler. Even if you are lucky enough to get past the sternum and rib cage and find the heart floating around there somewhere, it's still a good idea to cut off their head," Jax said.

"If vampires are dead, or undead, whatever the hell the term is, why does damaging the heart kill them? Does their heart still beat?"

"Yes, it still beats. Blood is an essential element for vampires. If it didn't continue to pump through their veins, they'd become more like a decaying corpse or a zombie than something that looks almost alive."

I wanted to ask a follow up about zombies but knew it was more important to stay on task with vampires for the moment. Plus, I really didn't want to know if zombies were real, also.

"Do you become a vampire from being bit?" I asked, immediately thinking about Brittany and the marks on what was left of her neck.

"No, you have to drink a vampire's blood. That's the only way to turn into one of them."

"What about holy water or a cross?" More movie tropes popped into my head.

"A cross would work great if you plan on stabbing them in the heart with it. Holy water also works great...if you are trying to wash your hands. Useless against vampires," he said making himself laugh.

"So the books and movies are pretty much full of shit," I said.

"Bram Stoker was pretty dead on," Jax replied. "Rumor has it he was a hunter, and *Dracula* was an autobiography. He put himself in the guise of Van Helsing. Stoker documented his hunt for an Alpha, leaving it as a bible for us to learn from."

"Wait," I said, not believing my ears. "Dracula was real?"

"Stoker renamed his alpha. Dracula was a cool name, especially with the legend of Vlad the Impaler attached to it. I'm sure its real name was something typical, like a Heinrich, but that wouldn't have sold nearly as many books."

I had to force my jaw closed. My mind was officially blown at that point. Not only were vampires real, but Dracula (or something like him) was real. I had to ask the obvious question. "What else is real?"

"What do you mean?" Jax asked.

"A few days ago, vampires didn't exist in my world. What else didn't exist but actually does? Werewolves? Fairies? Evil garden gnomes? I don't need a full list, but what else is out there?"

"Well, we primarily hunt vampires," he started.

"Primarily?" I interrupted.

"Werewolves exist. Although you were joking when you asked the other day, Niki was not when she answered you. Werewolves are real, but they do a good job of policing themselves. Most see lycanthropy as an affliction and take steps to curb it. Full moons can be rough for them, especially new werewolves, but like wolves, they run in a pack and work together.

"Fairies? Well, if you want something that sparkles in the sunlight, they do. Don't make one angry, or they all come after you. And they have very sharp teeth.

"As for the evil garden gnomes...I haven't personally seen one, but I heard tale."

"Now you are feeding me bullshit," I said.

We both laughed.

"If you are done with your breakfast," Jax said, "it's time to start combat training."

"Combat training?"

"Oh, come on, Sergeant. This should be old hat for you."

I stood from the table. "I don't want to hurt you, boss man."

"I'll take my chances," he said, standing from the table himself.

20

A large wrestling mat sat at the back of the warehouse. Collegiate wrestling mats were forty-two feet square. This looked smaller. Possibly a high school mat. A sparring dummy sat off to one side of the mat along with a rack of gloves, wooden swords, and wooden knives.

"I bought one of those at Medieval Times once," I said, pointing at the rack.

"Hopefully, you practiced with it. If so, I should be in for a world of hurt this morning." Jax strolled to the rack and grabbed a wooden knife by the hilt. He spun it in his hand a few times, obviously very comfortable with it. "Knife or sword?"

"I'll take a sword."

Jax selected one from the rack and tossed it to me. I snagged it out of the air, then proceeded to spin it under my arm and twirl it around in front of me as if I was fencing.

"This seems a little short," I said.

"It's the same size as a machete. They're easier to conceal than huge broad swords. Better to practice with what we will actually use in battle; wouldn't you agree, Sergeant?" Jax kicked off his shoes and stepped onto the mat. He held the much smaller knife out in front of him, ready to fight.

I nodded, spun the wooden machete in the air, removed my shoes, and entered the arena. My weapon had a longer reach to it. This really wasn't going to be fair. I expected to be stiff and rusty, but it wouldn't take long to loosen up and find my groove.

"Shouldn't we be wearing protective padding?"

Jax stood a few feet from me and smiled. "There's no padding in the field. Come on, Mike. Afraid to feel a little pain?"

I shifted my stance and turned my neck from side to side, cracking it in both directions. "A little pain? No. But I don't want to hurt..."

Before I could finish, Jax dropped to the ground, spun his legs, and swept my feet out from under me. I stared up at the vaulted warehouse ceiling with an ache in my back from where I had slammed into the mat. The point of his wooden knife pressed against the side of my throat. Fuck, he was quick for an old man.

"Ow, that fucking hurt."

"And you're dead," he said. He stood up and extended his arm to help me.

I grasped it and stood back up.

"That was a cheap shot. I didn't know we had started."

"Vampires, well creatures in general, rarely give warning to their prey. The moment you stepped onto the mat, stepped into my lair, you were fair game."

"Point taken." I rubbed the back of my head and shifted my feet back into a ready stance.

Jax took position across from me. With blazing fast speed, he rushed at me again. This time, I maneuvered out of the way, avoiding his swipe at my legs. Instead, he popped my arm with the wooden knife, punched me in the stomach, and shoved the knife under my chin.

"And you're dead," he said again.

I doubled over, holding my stomach, and coughed. I hadn't been punched like that in a very long time.

"Again," he said.

I straightened back up. Without warning, Jax grabbed me by the arm, spun me over his back, and drove me into the mat. Immediately, all the air left my lungs, and the wooden blade flew out of my hand. He held me on the ground in an arm bar.

"And you're dead."

Jax rolled away from me and popped back onto his feet.

I rolled onto my knees and sat up, refilling my lungs with oxygen. I held my hand out in front of me and coughed. Jax smirked and paced from one side of the mat to the other, giving me time to find my breath.

"How are you feeling, Mike?"

"Rusty," I answered and slowly rose onto my feet again. I shuffled over to my wooden machete and picked it up. "Why do I even have this in my hand?"

"How else are you going to take my head off?"

I bobbed my head. "Fair point."

"Are you ready to not die this time?"

"At some point, you'd think so."

Instead of waiting for Jax, I rushed at him with the machete in front of me. He didn't move and let the wooden tip hit him in his chest. He then hit me in the stomach, again, and swept my feet out from under me. I faceplanted into the mat, bouncing off my head.

"Ow," I said, lying with my cheek against the cold mat. "That one hurt. Also, not fair. I killed you first."

Jax bent down next to me. He grabbed my hand still holding the machete and twisted it so that the wooden blade pressed against his neck. "Take off the head." He turned my hand so the wood touched his torso. "Not stab in the chest." He stood up.

"You said piercing the heart works." I pushed myself up and rolled onto my butt.

He tapped his chest where I stabbed him. "That's not where the heart is. Taking off the head is easier. There's a lot of chest here, and the heart is a small target." He touched his head, then his chest. "Big head, small heart."

"That's an understatement," I said as I massaged the side of my face, tender from bouncing off the mat.

"Ready for some more, Sergeant White?" He held his hand out in front of me.

I grasped it and rose to my feet. "Why the hell not." With my feet planted, I stood at the ready.

21

The seven of us sat around the conference table in the large workspace. I sat across from Nate and Niki with Jax at one end of the table and Scott at the other. Thomas sipped blood from a wine glass as if was a fine wine. Knowing the thought of him drinking blood turned my stomach, I would swear he purposefully sat where it was easy for me to see him. Thomas was also the only one not eating pizza Josh ordered for lunch. Empty boxes littered the table.

"So Mike," Niki said. She pointed to me holding an ice pack against a growing bruise next to my eye, then pointed to Jax who didn't have a mark on him. "How did combat training with the boss go?"

I lowered the ice pack and rubbed my sore eye, trying not to wince from the stiffness in my arms as I did it. "I'll chalk that up to being a little rusty. I haven't had to do much sparring driving a forklift around. Granted, he's pretty fast for being an old man."

"Hear that, boss," Niki said to Jax. "Sergeant White thinks you're old."

From the end of the table, Jax laughed. "He's not wrong," he said. "With a little work, he may get close to hitting me. He actually had a shot or two that came within a foot of me. He'll be fine for the raid tonight." He gave a half smile and went back to his lunch.

"Tonight's raid? Two in two days?" Scott asked before anyone else had the opportunity.

"Yeah," Jax said. "We need to act fast. I want to take out Silas's dens as fast as he builds them. We've never been this close to him before. For some reason, he's decided to stick around. Thomas and I would've expected him to move already, but he hasn't. I plan to use this to our advantage. We'll find Silas and kill him before he decides to move to the next city."

Another raid! Tonight! My training had only just begun. After getting my ass handed to me by Jax, I knew I was out of practice if things turned into a hand-to-hand combat. At least my shooting accuracy wasn't off. As anxious as I was to find and kill Silas, I felt nervous at the thought of going into a vampire lair. Almost having my head bitten off by a twelve-year-old in bloodlust can put things into perspective.

"Don't worry," Jax said, noticing my surprise. "You'll be with me."

"What's the location for tonight?" Josh asked, sliding over to his computer.

"Farmhouse just outside of town." Jax gave him the address.

Josh typed it into the computer and pulled up a map. He pressed a button on the keyboard, and the printer sprang to life, spitting out an aerial map for each of us. Once done, he grabbed the printouts and slid them across the table. We each took a copy.

"One house and a barn?" Nate asked.

"Yes," Jax said. "Single story. Fairly secluded. Shouldn't have to worry with police response for this one. One team will take the house, and the other the barn. Thomas, something wrong?"

Everyone turned to Thomas. He had a pained look on his face while staring at the printout. "This would be unusual for him," he said. "Silas prefers the city. He thrives on crowds, the energy he gets from walking unseen amongst his prey. Secluded is unlike him. How sure is this?"

"Intel has tracked two different vampires to this location," Jax said.

"Just use an abundance of caution. I haven't seen this location myself. Jax, you know my preference is to have been there first," said Thomas.

"Our advantage is the fledglings don't know your face. I can't have you at every location, especially as fast as we are having to act. I don't know what your brother..."

"Do not call him that!" Thomas screamed at Jax. His eyes turned red, and he brandished his sharp fangs.

We all sat in stunned silence.

Thomas took a deep breath and recomposed himself; his eyes went back to the deep, almost black color, and his fangs disappeared into his jawline. "My apologies."

"That was my fault," Jax said. "I know how you feel about that. Neither Intel nor I know what Silas is up to. It looks like he's building an army, not just feeding. He's making new vampires at an alarming rate; way faster than the Council allows. We have to get ahead of him. Cut this off at the source."

"We don't know where Silas actually is?" I asked.

"He's constantly moving," Thomas answered. "He doesn't stay at a hive he creates. He has a beta he places there as a lieutenant. He then shuffles any new fledglings into that location, letting the lieutenant control them."

"Very efficient design. Reminds me of the military," I said.

"He's able to create his army and be an arm's length away from them," Nate chimed in. "The closest we've come to Silas was when he attacked you, and Niki and I were there. Fortunately, he decided to escape, probably thinking Thomas was with us. If he stuck around, who knows if we'd be sitting here eating pizza."

"Eat up..." Jax started.

My ring tone interrupted him before he could continue. I glanced at the caller ID and saw "Asshole" on the screen. I clicked the button to send Detective John Jennings to voice mail. The last thing I wanted to hear was some lame crap about investigating me, or don't take the law into my own hands. If only he knew the whole truth. I'm sure he'd rather I handle this than him.

"Everything ok?" Jax asked.

"Yes, sorry," I answered. "The detective investigating Brit's murder. He's probably making sure I'm still in town so he can blame me for it."

"Makes sense," he said. "Well, like I was saying, finish eating up and get some rest. We'll roll out at nineteen hundred."

After a few minutes of everyone grabbing the few remaining slices of pizza—except Thomas who continued to sip his glass of (*wine, it's wine*)—I turned toward Niki and Nate.

"Niki, how did a sweet Aussie like yourself get wrangled into vampire killing?"

Before she could answer, Thomas stood. "I'll leave you to your reminiscing. Jax, I'll see you in time for tonight's raid." He finished off his glass, placed it on the table near me, and stormed out the back of the warehouse.

I stared at the glass and saw the remaining remnants of blood that hung to the inside of the glass. It slowly began to pool at the bottom. The reddish tint of the glass faded as the pool grew to a small puddle. My stomach turned. "Something I said?" I asked the group.

"No," Nate said. "It's not you. He doesn't like to stick around long if we start talking about BNC."

"BNC?" I asked.

"Before Night Crew," Nate continued. "Thomas prefers to know as little about us as possible."

"Any idea why? I knew everything about the guys in my unit. Made us stronger together."

"That's true," Jax said. "But to Thomas, we're fragile. We die, and he doesn't. He's worked with countless teams. No one is still alive. If he gets close, he gets hurt."

Everyone sat there in silence for a moment. Although the others already knew it, I could tell from their expression it hit home each time they heard it. Thomas lived a lonely existence. He was surrounded by people he worked with and fought with. Surrounded by people who he saved when he could and felt the sting of their death when he couldn't. And through all of that, his main antagonist was his brother. Family. Blood. His own brother either killed or made vampires who killed the family Thomas chose. He lived a Shakespearean existence.

"How old are Thomas and Silas?"

"We don't know," Niki said. "And good luck trying to get that out of Thomas. He keeps his life very private, especially from before he turned."

"I can understand that. Jax, you have to have a ballpark at least?" I asked.

Jax leaned forward. "He's never told me exactly, but we've had enough conversations that I've picked up an idea. Let's just say he was a British citizen but born on the east coast."

"You mean pre-American Revolution?"

Jax nodded.

What amazing things Thomas must have seen over his long life! He saw technology go from the cotton gin to the telegraph to the Internet. He witnessed the evolution of warfare and its machinations from the musket rifle to automatic weapons. Did he stay in the background through history, or has he been an active participant? What I wouldn't give to pick Thomas's brain!

"Enough gossiping," Jax said. "I thought this was the Night Crew and not the ladies' social. Sorry, Niki. No offense."

"None taken. Although you should hear Nate gossip," she said. She stood and wrapped her arms around his large torso. "There's an old lady at a beauty salon somewhere inside this sculpted physique." She kissed him on the cheek and smiled to everyone. "Bedtime."

Nate stood up next to Niki, and they went to an office in the back that had been converted into a small bedroom.

"Nineteen hundred?" I asked Jax.

"Nineteen hundred," he said. He rose from the table, stretched, and started for a room.

"Jax," I said standing, turning his direction. "One more thing has been bothering me that I wanted to talk to you about."

"What is it?" he asked.

"It was something Silas said when he jumped me outside of Club Starlight. He told me he'd been waiting a long time to see me again."

"He saw you the night he killed your wife," he said.

"Yeah, but that was only a few days before. He said a long time," I told him.

"Maybe you two have crossed paths before, and he took a liking to you."

"I've searched back through my memory; he's not in there."

"Searched back through your memory?" Jax asked.

I glanced over and realized Scott and Josh still sat at the table finishing their pizza. They watched and listened intently as we had our conversation.

"I haven't mentioned it, but I have a gift. My brain does this weird thing where I can remember everything. Faces, events, words that were said; everything down to the smallest detail. That's how I knew to go to Club Starlight. I thought back and remembered Silas had their stamp on his hand."

"Don't they call that an eidetic memory?" Scott chimed in.

"Typically, an eidetic memory can recall just images well. I have that and what's called Highly Superior Autobiographical Memory. I remember everything in my life, except for one incident when I was ten. I had this friend...Martin. He and I were goofing around somewhere outside of town. I remember we rode our bikes there, then the next thing I knew, we were being loaded into the backs of ambulances. Later, my parents told me Martin didn't make it. They asked... the police asked... everyone asked me what happened. I didn't know. It was like a film had been erased. Only thing I could remember was a feeling. A feeling like I could have saved him but didn't. That feeling drove me to join the military, by the way."

"Sorry to hear about your friend," Josh said. "Losing a kid that young is terrible." His eyes shot to the back office where Nate and Niki had gone.

"But Silas doesn't show up anywhere in that steel trap of yours?" Jax asked, pointing at my head.

"Not at all," I said. Although I wondered if something with Silas was trying to get out of my head. The flashes from the other night came to mind. I heard Martin's screams when he transformed in front of me. It was almost like my Ultranet tried to find Silas's face, almost did, but then timed out.

"Well, at some point," Jax said, "I think he saw you. Let me see what Intel has on Silas's movements. In the meantime, get some rest. This old man needs a nap."

22

Jax's SUV turned off the main highway onto a gravel road. I drove the second, staying a few hundred yards behind him. The dust kicked up from the lead car made visibility tough.

We were a few miles outside of town. Close enough to still be considered part of the city, but far enough away to be quiet and secluded, just like the map showed. The woods crowded the small gravel road, blocking out even the full moon that sat above us. We stayed on the road, twisting and turning, for a mile.

We still didn't have a view of the farmhouse when Jax pulled over and killed the lights to his vehicle. I pulled in behind him and turned mine off as well. He stepped out of the driver's seat and headed to me. I rolled my window down. The GPS said we were a half mile from the house.

"What's wrong?" I asked.

The dust from the road still settled, and I resisted the urge to cough from breathing it in.

"We're walking the rest of the way," he said. "That'll give us more of the element of surprise. I don't want us pulling up in front of the house just to see vampires scurrying into the woods. We'd be the ones hunted at that point."

"Makes sense," I said.

Scott stepped out of the car. I rolled up the window, opened the door, and stepped out as well. Scott and I stepped to the rear of the car. He opened the trunk and grabbed cases of equipment.

Nate, Niki, and Thomas joined us from the other SUV. As they did, I turned around to get a better look at where we were. With the only light coming from the interior of the SUV, I could barely see anything. The road was just large enough for one car to pass down. Two would've been a struggle, especially as close as the trees were to the edge of the road. In the dark, everything felt claustrophobic. A chilled breeze blew through the trees. The branches occasionally moved in the wind creating loud cracking noises in the silence of the woods.

Nate and Scott passed out equipment to everyone. Niki and Jax were both handed shotguns. Niki strapped her silver whip to her hip. Everyone reached for a machete. I grabbed the 9mm from yesterday and tucked it into a holster on my side. Nate opened another case containing ear buds, and we all took one.

I put mine in my right ear. Immediately, the sound around me amplified. I heard a culmination of sound from everyone's earpiece in my right ear. No longer was there silence among the woods. The tree limbs cracking in the wind sounded thunderous.

"Everyone online?" Josh asked.

"We hear ya, love," Niki said.

"Great. Who's getting my eyes in the air?" Josh asked.

"Working on it, now," Scott said.

I glanced over at Scott as he unlatched a large, hard shell case. He tossed the lid up on its hinges. The inside of the case was lined with black foam padding. He pulled out a large drone with four blades, one on each side, and placed it on the ground next to the SUV.

"Ready for you," Scott said.

The blades of the quadcopter fired up, sending a whining noise through the woods that echoed off the trees. The drone rose a few feet in the air, hovered a few seconds, turned, then shot into the darkness above us.

"I see you," Josh said.

"That sounds creepy," Niki commented.

Scott closed the lid of the drone case and pulled another one to the edge of the trunk. He opened it, and flashlights lay in rows.

"Grab one," Jax said. After everyone but Thomas reached in, he said, "Does everyone have what you need?"

We all nodded. We were each armed as if heading to battle. Between the six of us, we held over a dozen blades or guns, not counting the silver grenades. Thomas was the lone exception. He only had a machete that dangled off his hip inside his long coat.

"Thomas," I asked. "Nothing else for you?"

"I can see without the use of a flashlight," he said. "And I protect myself without the gun."

"Good to know," I said.

"Josh," Jax said, reverberating inside of my earpiece, "how are we look-ing? Are we clear from here to the house?"

"The trees are making it hard to see from the ground level but using heat sigs, I'm only seeing the five bright reds and one light blue from you guys. I'll scan the house and barn when you arrive. For now, I'll keep an eagle eye on your path."

Jax gathered us together. "Lord, protect us from evil as we deliver Your judgment to them. Amen."

"Amen," we all said in unison.

"Thomas, you take lead. Keep flashlights off for now."

With Thomas taking point, we began the half mile walk to the farm-house and the barn. With the darkness making my eyesight nonexistent, my hearing picked up every sound. Through my earpiece, I could hear everyone breathing. I felt my heart beating in my head. The wind con-tinued to send a chill through the air, blowing through the trees. The cracking of branches screamed into the night. Every step on the gravel road crunched beneath our feet, echoing into the darkness.

Finally, the woods eased their grip, and the moonlight broke through to illuminate the farmhouse. A front porch wrapped around it, and the door sat in the middle of the house with two windows on either side. Bathed in the moonlight, it looked like a painting sitting in the clearing with the barn next to it. An older model Chevy truck was parked between the house and the barn.

"Mike with me. We'll take the barn," Jax whispered. "Nate and Scott, take the house. Niki, watch the front. Thomas, circle around back and watch the house and barn. Josh, what do your eyes see?"

"You're still clear. I'm not picking up a heat signature inside the house, but that doesn't mean anything. Cold-blooded blood suckers don't put off a lot of heat. No offense, Thomas. You know I love you."

Jax and I slowly walked to the barn. We stayed next to the tree line before crouching down in the clearing. From the corner of my eye, I saw Scott and Nate doing the same thing, heading to the house.

"Approaching the barn," Jax said.

"Entering the house," Nate replied.

I stayed just behind Jax on his right side. We stepped up to a small white door in the front of the large red barn. The larger barn door stood to our right. Jax had the sling of his shotgun around his shoulder, and the flashlight held directly in front of him. I held the 9mm in my hand with my flashlight cupped below it. We both had the machetes sheathed on our hips. He pointed to the door, then our flashlights. I understood what he meant.

Jax slowly turned the doorknob, and then quickly threw open the door. We both ignited our flashlights and moved inside the door. The flashlights lit up the interior of the barn.

A large John Deere tractor sat in the middle of the barn just beyond the closed barn door. Tractor implements sat on the far side against the outside wall. Stalls filled with hay lined the inside of the barn. Our flashlights drifted across red wood separating the various stalls. Rusty nails protruded from the wood slats, and cobwebs blanketed the walls. The air was thick with the smell of grass, dirt, and manure. I could taste the stench in the air.

Jax had moved over by the tractor, keeping his light dancing in front of him. He pointed his flashlight up, and we saw a loft above us. He motioned for me to investigate.

I searched around me and found the ladder. It sat a few feet in front of me. The only sound I heard was my footsteps crunching the dried hay beneath my feet as I crept to the ladder. I faintly heard the sound of boards creaking in my ear. That must have been from Nate or Scott walking on the hardwood floor of the house.

I grabbed the wooden ladder. I tugged on it to make sure it was still solid. Nothing broke, but I did send dirt and dust raining on top of me and coughed in response. The sound echoed in the silent barn. I placed the flashlight in my pants' pocket, sending a beam of light directly above me illuminating the dust slowly descending. I gripped the rungs of the ladder and scaled to the top.

As my head broke the plane of the loft, I pulled the flashlight out of my pocket and quickly shined it around. I finished my climb to the top and stood on the second floor. With the exception of large spider webs and their accompanying spiders, the loft was empty. Dust and dirt lined the floor.

"Nothing up here," I said. "I think the barn's empty."

"I agree," Jax said.

I directed my beam of light to the bottom floor and found him almost to the back wall by the tractor equipment.

"Status reports," Jax ordered.

"Outside is quiet," Niki said.

"Nothing in the house so far," Scott said.

"Kitchen's empty, including the fridge," Nate added. "Doesn't look like anyone's been here for a while. Vamp or human."

"I've not heard or seen anything," Thomas chimed in.

"Wait," Nate said. "There's a basement door...and it stinks."

"Pause, Nate," Jax said. "Mike, get down and head to the house. Help provide cover. Niki, I'm heading your way."

I turned back to the ladder, ducking to avoid a large spider web built in the corner. My descent down the ladder went quicker than my ascent up. Jax met me back at the door.

"Run to the house. Niki and I will provide cover if needed." Jax went through the door and jogged toward Niki.

I followed him and turned to the house. I sprinted from the barn door, past the clearing and the old Chevy truck, to the porch steps, and finally up to the front door. I pictured vampires waiting in the darkness, ready to leap out at me if I slowed down. Although Jax and Niki had my cover, and we hadn't seen any sign of a vampire yet, my anticipation level was on high alert.

Stepping in through the front door, I felt the stillness of the house. The air felt stale. The door opened into the living room on my right, and a dining room on my left. A layer of dust had settled on the coffee table in the middle of the living room. The TV and TV stand next to the wall were also covered in dust. On the hardwood floor, I saw the faint footprints of Nate and Scott's shoes. The beam of light from my flashlight highlighted the falling dust bunnies, kicked up by Nate and Scott, as they made their way back to the floor.

Whoever had lived here had been gone for a while.

"Mike, back this way," Nate said. His voice simultaneously came from my left and was in my right ear.

I kept my flashlight dancing around the room as I walked. A floral-patterned wallpaper decorated the dining room. A wooden table with four chairs sat in the middle. Pictures hung on the wall. Each picture contained three smiling people: dad, mom, and daughter. The daughter's age differed between pictures; she was young in a few of them, but a teenager in others.

Why didn't they take the pictures with them?

Crossing the dining room, I stepped into the kitchen. The sink sat on the left side of the long kitchen with an island in the middle. Just beyond the island, Nate and Scott stood by a closed door.

As I stepped past the island, the smell Nate mentioned hit me. Even through the closed door, the smell emanated out of it.

"Mike's here," Scott said.

"Open the door," Jax said in our ears.

Nate turned the doorknob and threw open the door. The smell of death and rotting decay intensified. The whole kitchen became entrenched in it. The urge to vomit immediately rose up in my throat. I struggled to push it back down.

Along with the smell, I heard a humming noise coming up from the basement.

"What the fuck is that noise?" Scott whispered. He took a step closer to the door and listened.

Flies! Flies billowed out. Hundreds of flies. They swarmed out of the door as we batted them away from our faces.

Scott grabbed two glow sticks from his back pocket and cracked them. His face and hands glowed green. He tossed them into the cellar. I pushed my way through the flies and the smell of death to peer into the basement. The light sticks bounced off a step and landed ten feet down. I saw a hand and long hair lying on the floor.

Nate and Scott glanced at each other before holding their fists out in front of them. "Rock, paper, scissors, shoot," they said in unison, followed by Nate saying, "Shit."

"Enjoy," Scott said with a smirk on his face.

"Fine. Mike, you're with me," Nate said. "Joys of being the new guy."

Nate took the first few steps through the door and down the rickety wooden stairs. He held his flashlight in one hand and the other on the grip of his shotgun. The steps groaned as his large frame descended.

I followed a few steps behind him, staring at the hand and long hair laying at the bottom. My foot cautiously found each step as I eased myself down into the dark basement. The further down I went, the more of the floor I could see.

After a few steps, I saw the hair and hand attached to a body. I recognized the face when I saw it: the teenage girl from the pictures. She lay dead on the floor. Her chest lay against the dirt floor and back faced the ceiling. Her head, though, had been completely turned around backward, and her neck was ripped open. I didn't know how her head stayed attached to her body with the amount of trauma. Grayish white bone peeked through the dried blood and tissue.

I stared at her body while descending the last few steps. The beam of my flashlight illuminated my path, while her body was washed in the sick green glow of the light sticks. Just before I reached the bottom step, I heard Nate.

"Holy shit!" he said. "They were bled!"

My gaze raised from the steps to directly in front of me. I brought the flashlight up with them, but Nate's light was already there.

Two bodies hung from the rafters of the basement. I didn't need my flashlight to make out who they were. The daughter lay on the floor with her head nearly ripped off, and mom and dad dangled from the ceiling by their ankles. Both bodies had been stripped naked. Cuts and slashes covered them from head to toe. I noticed something else on a few areas. On their legs, arms, and neck, small incisions were made, and surgical tubing had been inserted into these incisions and into their veins. White pus dripped from the end of the tubing.

They never took the pictures because they never left the house.

I stopped moving on the next to last step, staring at the bodies suspended two dozen feet away from me. The open wounds and rotting flesh crawled with flies. I glanced down at their daughter lying on the floor. The flies invaded her neck. The dead flesh bubbled and moved on her body.

I realized why when I looked back up at her parents. I had mistaken the drip from the tubing as white pus. Instead, maggots dropped from the end of the tubes. Their skin crawled with them, moving in and out of the open gashes. The same with the daughter's neck. They squirmed just beneath her skin, making the flesh ripple.

Between the smell, the flies, and the sight of maggots invading the bodies, I couldn't take it anymore. I turned around and ran up the stairs as fast as I could. I clenched my mouth closed with my hand as tight as possible, pushing past Scott who had just started his descent. I sprinted past the basement door, past the kitchen and dining room, and out the front door. Just as I cleared the wrap around porch, I doubled over and vomited. It felt like I threw up everything I had ever eaten.

As my head hung between my knees, I prayed I could keep the image of the crawling, dead flesh from making it into my Ultranet. *Please God, don't let me relive that image again.*

Niki and Jax walked to me as Scott and Nate finally left the house through the front door. I moved over to the porch and collapsed onto my ass.

"Don't worry, love," Niki said. "We've all done it. Main reason we keep water in the trucks."

"Where are they?" Nate asked.

"Josh, any word from Intel?" Jax asked. "Thomas, are you seeing anything?"

Thomas appeared from the side of the house passing next to the old truck. "This place has been abandoned. They fed on the girl and bled the parents. They died before his wife." He pointed at me.

"Jax," Josh said in our ears, "Intel doesn't have anything new. Just what they confirmed earlier."

"We know they'd been here, but not recently. Intel has bad info."

"This doesn't feel right," Thomas said. "I told you earlier, I don't like not seeing a place firsthand."

"I know. Josh, drone sweep. Anything?"

"One second."

There was a long pause as we all waited to hear back from Josh. No one let their guard down. Everyone stayed standing but me. The only sound I heard was the faint, high-pitched sound of the drone's blades as it flew high above us.

Finally, Josh said, "All clear. I'm landing the drone. Battery is running low. Scott, can you carry me back?"

"I hate it when you phrase it like that," Scott said.

The sound of the drone's four blades grew louder as it descended in front of us. It landed a few yards away, and the blades stopped spinning.

"Mike, are you good to walk back?" Jax asked.

"My head isn't spinning anymore. It's only a half mile. I'll be fine," I said.

"Then let's head out."

Scott grabbed the drone, and we marched back. This time we had our flashlights on and didn't care if we made noise. We didn't need to maintain the element of surprise. The place had been empty.

I hoped to not go on many raids with the Night Crew. Just enough to track down Silas and get my revenge for what he did to Brittany. My first "real" raid and instead of killing a vampire, I threw up in the front yard. Stellar example of my fortitude.

Within a few minutes, we made it back to the vehicles. Nate lowered the back of the SUV, and Scott loaded up the drone. Niki tossed me a bottle of water. I took a swig to rinse the taste of vomit, dust, and decay out of my mouth and spit. I downed the rest of the bottle in a few large gulps.

While I drank the water, Scott, Nate, Jax, and Niki loaded up their equipment into the hard-shell totes. Thomas sat in the front passenger seat of the first SUV again, waiting for everyone to finish. Nate, Niki, and Jax eventually joined him after they finished packing up their equipment, leaving Scott to latch the last of the totes.

"Hey, Scott," I hollered, walking to the back of the car after finishing my water. "Don't close up yet. I still have my gear."

The first SUV drove up next to us. "Go ahead," I said. "I know the way back from here. We won't be far behind you."

"See you in a bit," Niki yelled from the backseat. Their SUV started slowly down the dirt road, their tires kicking up a small cloud of dust.

Scott grabbed his own bottle of water and walked to the passenger door.

I opened the case and removed my earpiece. I dropped the clip from my 9mm and placed it inside a second case. "Look on the bright side," I hollered. "At least when we get back, we won't have any torching to do."

Scott didn't respond. I thought he would appreciate that but guess not. I sat my machete down in the trunk and closed the back. I heard a tree limb cracking. I turned my head from side to side, but didn't see Scott around the car.

"Hey Scott, if you needed to take a piss, you could've just said so," I yelled.

Behind me, I heard a loud shuffling of gravel. Before I could spin around, I felt a sharp sting of fire on the back of my neck. Immediately, every nerve in my body lit up. Waves of excruciating pain rushed over me. Every muscle clenched, and it felt like a jack hammer repeatedly hitting me. I dropped to the ground, convulsing.

My head slammed against the gravel road, and my eyes focused on the ground on the far side of the car. Scott lay there unnaturally still, his eyes not focused on anything. Someone grabbed his legs and dragged him away.

As my convulsions stopped, I tried to roll over and peer up at who attacked me. Before I could, another flash of pain exploded across my temple. My head bounced off the gravel again, and everything went dark.

23

"Mike," Brittany said. "Mike, I need you to wake up."

Her voice had such a sweet timbre to it. I loved listening to her.

"Mike!" she said, becoming more aggressive. She started to shake me awake. "Michael White, wake up!" she yelled.

As she yelled into my ear, my head slammed against something hard. My hands instinctively reached for my head, but they couldn't move. They were locked together behind my back. Slowly, I opened my eyes. The pain in my head hurt excruciatingly bad. Alex Van Halen was having a drum contest with Neil Peart inside my skull.

At first, I saw only blurry images. After repeatedly blinking and trying to reset my eyes, my vision cleared, and my senses started to come back to me. The memory of the last thing I saw, Scott being dragged away, came back.

I gazed around and found myself lying in the backseat of a car with my hands cuffed behind my back.

Still lying down, I couldn't make out the driver. The car bounced down an uneven road. I must've imagined the shaking to be Brittany shaking me awake, and my head bouncing off the door finally woke me up.

I planted my feet on the floorboard and pulled my torso up. The change in elevation sent a new wave of pain. It started from my lower back, up through my increasingly sore shoulders, past the sting of raw, burnt skin on the back of my neck, and finally exploded into the drum battle within my head.

"Welcome to the land of the living, sleepy head," a familiar voice said. "Do you know you call out for your dead wife while you sleep?"

"Jennings?" I asked. "I'm confused. What happened? Why am I handcuffed? Am I under arrest?"

After sitting up, I took a better look at my surroundings. I recognized this car. He was driving my car! I was handcuffed in the back of my own Acura!

"Detective, why are we in my car?"

"You are just filled with questions, aren't you?"

"I have a lot more where that came from, so why don't you start answering a few of them? Let's start with, why the fuck am I handcuffed in the backseat of my car!" I violently slammed against the back seat, trying to wiggle my hands underneath me or break free of my handcuffs somehow. I knew I'd seen people do this in the movies. Lying bastards.

"Well, I figure if both you and your car went missing, it would appear that you, after having killed your wife and knowing the police were closing in on you, decided to skip town. Go on the lam," he said.

I looked at the rear-view mirror. His eyes stared back at me. I held his gaze, not looking away, until he was forced to look back at the road. His face had a smirk on it that I couldn't wait to knock off.

A horrible thought came to me. I had to be wrong, because it couldn't have been the case. At this point, though, what did I have to lose?

"Are you taking me to Silas?" I asked.

His grin widened. The son of a bitch worked for Silas. Jax said Bram Stoker's Dracula was a fairly accurate account of hunting an alpha. Dracula had a human acquaintance, so why not Silas?

"You're a goddamn Renfield!" I shouted, throwing my back against the backseat again and kicking the back of the driver's seat.

"Let's not throw a temper tantrum," Jennings said, still with a smile across his face. "You should be honored. He wants you for himself. He's been looking for you for a long time. He came to your house to find you, but you weren't home, so he decided to have a snack instead."

The memory rushed back into my head. Silas kneeling over her mutilated body. Her heart beating its few remaining beats. The blood-soaked carpet. The gurgling noise as she died in my arms. Camp Anger again, here I come.

With the distraction of vampire hunting, I don't know if I was on the way to Camp Acceptance, but I knew right now I was firmly back in Camp Anger.

"Why didn't he kill me, then?" I screamed at him.

"You can ask him yourself soon enough," he shrugged.

The car bounced on the uneven back roads. According to the clock in the car, it was twenty-one hundred. I'd been out for maybe twenty minutes. Jennings was probably driving on these roads to avoid being noticed on the main highway.

"What do you get out of all this?"

"I get the gift of immortality, Sergeant White. I get blessed with living forever," he said reverently.

"You know he gives that shit away for free, right? Between my friends and I, we've killed a good number of so-called immortals." Well, *they* had. I kept one from biting my neck while Thomas killed it. Close enough for me. "I'd do air quotes around that word immortal, but my hands are occupied right now. It seems immortality isn't all it's cracked up to be. Lose your head, and it's done. Sounds to me like you're just a shitty Highlander with a taste for blood."

I had my own smirk on my face now. I could tell from the rear-view mirror I was making him angry this time. Camp Anger has T-shirts if you'd like one.

"I get to be a leader in his army," he said frustrated.

"Good luck with that. Plus, when the rest of the Crew realize I'm not back, they'll hunt down every last blood sucker."

"Don't count too much on the rest of your Night Crew. Your friend who was with you is already dead," he bragged.

"You killed Scott!" I hollered at him. I lost my smile and kicked the back of the seat again.

"The rest are being taken care of as we speak. We appreciate your help in finding their headquarters. They'd been a pain in Silas's side for too long."

"Helping you find them?" Just as I asked, my Ultranet kicked into gear. My head flashed back to Jennings showing up at my hotel room yesterday. I thought he came there to be an asshole and pressure me into confessing that I killed Brittany.

Sitting in the back of my car, I closed my eyes and sank into the memory. He had something in his hand when he sat on the couch next to my jacket. He very subtly played with it between his fingers. When Jennings stood back up, though, he didn't have it. The detective came all the way to my hotel to place a tracker on my jacket. Silas knew Nate and Niki saved me and would try to recruit me, and he had Jennings track me.

I opened my eyes. "Are they dead already?"

"No, not yet," Jennings said. The smile crept back onto his face. "Silas wants to bleed them."

The vision of the parents strung up in the basement of the house splashed across my head. This time, though, the faces changed to be Jax's, Niki's, and Nate's. They dangled from a rafter, slices taken out of their skin and tubing shoved into their main arteries to bleed them faster.

"Why not just kill them?"

"Silas always says the two sweetest vintages are young boys and hunters."

Martin's screams in the tunnel echoed back into my head. Those red eyes floating in the darkness, just outside the reach of the sunlight.

Jennings continued. "He wants them to suffer. He's going to take his time with them. Bleed them slowly to get every ounce of hunter blood. Silas is going to make them the main dish at his party. Think of them as being on tap."

His lips spread wide, almost like he was the Joker. The look on Jennings's face was one of pure excitement, almost to the point of ecstasy. Between the darkness of the road and the dashboard lights, his eyes screamed of lunacy. In the book, Renfield had been institutionalized. I didn't think Jennings was far removed from that.

Mike, I heard a voice say.

Brittany? I closed my eyes to imagine her next to me. *I'm in deep shit, Honey. I don't know how I'm going to get out of this one.*

Mike, what did you always bitch about me doing?

Bitch about you doing? I loved you.

Stop with the rose-colored glasses shit just because I'm dead. We fought just like any normal couple, and I did things that annoyed the shit out of you. Use that amazing brain of yours and get your ass out of here. Now, what did you complain about me doing?

With my eyes still closed, and her sitting right next to me, she flicked her fiery red hair right in front of my face. Her hair that always draped so beautiful around her shoulders. I loved brushing the hair back from her face. It annoyed the crap out of her when it didn't all fit in a ponytail. She had so many bobby pins always...

Thanks, Brit.

The bastard had me in the same car Brittany and I had gone everywhere in. Every time I cleaned out the car, I'd find two dozen bobby pins. More than once, I had come home and asked, "How do you get them in the backseat if you don't even sit back there?"

"Bobby Pin Gnomes?" she had responded jokingly. "Those things can travel." She had known I hated finding them all over the place.

"Sergeant," Jennings said. "Did you pass out on me? I was enjoying our conversation."

I ignored him. My hands used their limited mobility to search the seat cushion. I hadn't cleaned the car out for months. There had to be a bobby pin or twelve in here somewhere. I dropped my shoulders down to give my hands more reach. Of course, my shoulders screamed at the pain, which didn't help the ongoing drum roll in my head.

My hands slipped between the bottom and back cushions. I could feel trash that had made its way down here, and something that felt like a quarter. My fingers brushed the rough carpet. Finally, they hit against a thin piece of metal. Using my fingernail, I scraped it closer. A bobby pin!

I grasped the bobby pin in my fingers and eased the strain on my shoulders. I removed my hands from inside the seat cushion with the pin still between my fingers.

With my eyes still closed, I searched my Ultranet. While in Afghanistan, I got into an argument with Austin about how easily you can get out of handcuffs. He said they were simple, and I felt if they were so easy, why do cops use them all the time. He pulled up a YouTube video where a guy picked the lock on a pair using multiple items, including a bobby pin. Austin had tried and tried to do it but couldn't recreate what the guy did. We left him handcuffed to a pole the better part of the afternoon. He swore he could get out. Somehow, this man was now part of military intelligence.

I recalled that YouTube video in my head. I watched the guy bend the bobby pin, flatten the end of it, insert it into the lock, and click! I followed along, imitating his steps. I prayed I'd have better luck than Austin. With the pin bent and inserted into the lock, I started jiggling the pin to get it further in the lock.

"Mike, are you alive back there?" Jennings hollered to me. "Silas isn't going to reward me if you're dead." He reached his right hand back to me and hit my leg. "Mike!"

With his hand still next to my leg, I reached my newly freed hands around and grabbed his arm.

"What the fuck!" he screamed.

The car swerved as I pulled his arm back, bending his shoulder the wrong way. He screamed in pain. I placed my foot on his arm, holding it in place and punched him in the face.

He completely let go of the steering wheel with his left hand and grabbed for something on the passenger side. Jennings raised it, and I saw the blue spark of the TASER he used on me earlier.

I lunged forward before he could use it on me again. We wrestled for the TASER while the car veered from one side of the road to the other. My right arm kept his arm outstretched with the TASER in it. His left hand tried to regain control of the car while mine continued punching him in the face from the backseat.

My right arm started to give way, while his started to curl to me. I could hear the TASER sparking and smell the ozone as it drew closer and closer.

Before he could touch me, I grabbed his right arm with both of mine and shoved the TASER into his neck. He convulsed behind the wheel, bouncing in place. His foot smashed on the gas pedal, causing the car to immediately accelerate. The wheel turned, and the car angled for the side of the road.

I quickly dropped down behind the driver's seat, my back to the car door, as the car plowed into the ditch. I felt the impact but was braced in between the backseat and the front.

With the car no longer moving, I reached behind me and opened the back door. I slid off the floorboard, crawling on the ground with my elbows until my feet finally fell onto the dirt. Standing, I moved to the front door. The detective's face had slammed into the steering wheel, and he was unconscious.

I opened the driver's side door and pulled him out of the car. My first instinct was to leave him unconscious in the ditch, but then I had a better idea. I placed the cuffs on him, grabbed his sidearm from his waist, and popped the trunk of the Acura. I dragged him over to the trunk, picked him up, and tossed him in.

When I finished loading him in the trunk, I rushed to the driver's seat. I needed to hurry and get to headquarters. Thankfully, the car started. I peeled out of the ditch and onto the road. I punched the gas pedal all the way to the floor. Hopefully I'd get back before Silas attacked.

24

The Acura's engine hummed. I skidded the tires and almost lost control when I turned off the backroad the detective had us on. I'd never driven the car that fast before, as I sped back onto the main highway. Fortunately, the road sat almost empty, or I would've plowed into anyone in the way. I passed a few cars as if they were standing still.

It felt like I levitated onto two wheels when I took the exit off the highway headed for downtown. I blew through every traffic light. Thank God, there was no one at the intersections. Fate had to be on my side.

As I sped closer to the entrance to our headquarters, I prayed I wasn't too late, but feared I was. The fenced gate sat slightly ajar, and the SUV idled in front of it. The doors to the SUV hung open, and the windows were smashed. The tires had been slashed, the hood bent open, and steam billowed out.

For the first time since jumping behind the wheel, I took my foot off the gas and slammed on the brake. The brakes locked up. Tires screeched. As the car rapidly decelerated, I cranked the wheel, sending gravel from the road onto the parked SUV. I punched the gas again and sped up through the fence to the building. Sparks flew from the side of the car as the gate scraped down it. I threw the car into park right at the front.

I hopped out and ran to the entrance. The solid metal door lay thrown on its side, ripped straight off the hinges. Seeing it tossed aside like that made me panic. How could we possibly stand up to a monster that could do that? The only thing I had on me was the detective's pistol. Like that would do any good against someone—*something*—that could rip a metal door off of its hinges. I knew Silas would've brought others along to attack HQ. He would've had an army.

With both hands on the gun raised to my shoulder, I stepped over the destroyed door. The inside was in absolute disarray. Shelving lay on the ground. Boxes of equipment and supplies littered across the warehouse floor.

I carefully walked through the rubble, listening for any sound. I had no idea if anyone was still here—friend or foe. Broken glass crunched under my feet with every step. Liquid, probably (*hopefully*) from water bottles, darkened the concrete floor. Above me, the remaining canister lights flickered. The strobe effect cast foreboding shadows through the whole warehouse.

Inside the meeting room where we sat for lunch just earlier today, the monitors lay shattered. Some were completely broken in two. The table had a machete buried halfway into it. Next to the table, I found a headless body. I took a deep breath. Fortunately, I didn't recognize the clothing and relaxed slightly, exhaling.

"Jax?" I hollered into the emptiness of the warehouse.

Just before I reached the hallway, I saw Josh's wheelchair tossed to one side. I picked it back up on its wheels, checking for blood. It was clean. "Josh?"

In the hallway toward the break room, the security lights provided the only light, washing everything in a deep, red hue. The glass from the fluorescent tubes covered the hall.

"Nate, Niki, Thomas?" I yelled.

A low moan emanated from the break room. I stopped to make sure my imagination wasn't playing a trick on me. Standing there with the handgun grasped between both hands, I listened. Finally, I heard the moan again. Someone needed help! I quickly rushed into the break room, not even caring that it could be a trap.

Thomas sat propped up on the floor next to the cabinets against the wall. I saw his shirt ripped apart, and large slashes across his chest. His arms were outstretched to either side of him. Each hand had a kitchen knife driven through it, nailing him to the cabinets like he was hung on a cross.

"Holy shit!" I yelled, almost sliding over to him as I sprinted into the room. I ripped out the first knife, then the second.

His arms dropped to his sides. His head hung limply.

"Thomas, how can I help?"

"Blood," he groaned back to me, barely audible. He was dying. Images of holding Brittany as she took her last breaths rushed into my head. I had to fight my own brain and focus on saving Thomas.

"Blood, of course," I said.

I stood and rushed to the fridge in the break room. I'd seen him put a bag in here earlier today. I remembered making sure to avoid that fridge so I wouldn't see a bag of blood lying next to our pizza leftovers.

"Dammit, nothing in here," I hollered to him. Sweat trickled into my eyes, and my heart raced. I wiped the sweat from my brow. "Where else do you keep it?"

He raised a hand and pointed to a back room. As quickly as he raised it, he dropped it back down. His hand looked like he had been struck with the stigmata. His wounds weren't healing. I was losing him.

I ran to the back room. As soon as I entered, I knew it wouldn't matter. My steps stuck to the drying blood on the floor. I left footprints walking to the refrigerator Thomas kept in here. A dozen bags had been ripped open and lay scattered everywhere.

I hurried back to the break room. "Anywhere else?" I asked.

Thomas shook his head. He placed a palm on the countertop above him and tried to pull himself up. He made it halfway up before collapsing back to the ground.

The thought of Brittany, her nightgown ripped open and chest pumping its last few attempts, flooded my head again. Another of Silas's victims was about to die in front of me. I couldn't let that happen again. Silas wasn't going to take someone else.

I went over to Thomas and bent down. I held my arm out in front of him. "Drink," I said. I tried to sound confident but knew I failed. I couldn't stand watching Thomas drink from a glass, yet now I was offering him my arm.

He pushed me away.

"Listen, you prideful son of a bitch. You don't have a choice. This is it. I'm going to kill him, but I can't without your help." I took a deep breath and steadied my voice. "Now, drink, dammit."

Thomas grabbed my arm and brought it close to his mouth.

"Be gentle," I said. "Don't kill me, and this stays between us."

In one sudden move, Thomas opened his mouth and buried his fangs into my arm. I felt a sharp burning sting like a hot poker pierced my skin, followed by a warm, flowing sensation. *That's blood. That's my blood.* He viciously grabbed my arm tighter and began squeezing it, pulling it further onto his fangs. I thought of how Silas held the girl outside of Club Starlight.

My head felt heavy on my shoulders. My stomach started to feel nauseous. I struggled to hold myself up. My legs gave way, and I collapsed onto the linoleum floor.

Thomas released his grip on my arm. I awkwardly pulled my shirt off with my other arm and wrapped it around the puncture wounds. I slowly scooted next to him and laid my back against the cabinets. My breathing was deep and slow. I felt like I'd just run a marathon.

Thomas raised his head. I could see the color starting to come back into his face. "So, was that as good for you as it was for me?"

"Thomas Price," I said in disbelief. I let a smile cross my face. "Did you just crack a joke after taking a quart of blood from me?"

He smiled and gave a brief chuckle. "I do have a sense of humor."

"News to me," I said.

"I can be quite the prankster when I want to be. Like sitting next to someone who can't stand the sight of me drinking blood."

"I knew you did that shit on purpose. Asshole," I said.

We both laughed until mine turned into a cough.

"What happened to you?" he asked.

I told him about Detective Jennings and what he had told me.

"What about here?" I asked.

"Let me show you," he said. He placed his index finger on my temple.

My head shot back suddenly against the cabinet, and my eyes strained to stay in their sockets. Although they were completely open, I wasn't seeing through mine anymore. I was seeing through Thomas's eyes.

25

Jax pulled the SUV to the front gate. Thomas sat in front while Niki sat curled into Nate in the back. The gate was shut, and Thomas could see the lock still attached to it.

"Hey, Niki," Jax said. "Do you mind sparing Nate for a brief moment so he can unlock the gate?"

"Of course. Get to work, beautiful," she told Nate.

Nate opened the car door, and slowly walked over to the gate.

Even though the engine was running and the windows were closed, Thomas could still hear the gravel under Nate's feet. Part of the curse of being a vampire, *Thomas thought. He tried to keep himself secluded and isolated as much as possible. Hearing everyone's footsteps, breathing, and even heart beats drove him mad. Inside of a closed canister made things worse. The sounds echoed inside the car.*

Thomas opened the door and stepped out into the night air.

"You ok?" Jax asked.

Thomas nodded and shut the door. He hesitated just outside the car for a moment, then meandered a few feet away. While he walked, he twisted his hands in front of him, feeling the air, soaking in the night. As an apex predator, he felt at home in the darkness. He loathed what he was and tried to find peace in the areas of his existence that he could. He preferred darkness and solitude. Hunting allowed him to use his skills for good after so many years of horror.

Behind him, Nate struggled with the gate. He unlatched the lock with no problem, but the gate itself felt stuck after opening only two feet.

Niki rolled her window down. "Having a problem, love?"

"It won't go any further," he said, frustratingly pulling on it. "It feels like the pole is bent."

"Keep straining those muscles, my Nubian prince. I'm going to sit here and be enticed by the view."

Thomas ignored their lovers' banter. The air bothered him. The temperature had fallen a degree, and the wind had stopped blowing. Everything went silent and still, and the calm caused every nerve ending of Thomas's body to fire.

From behind him, he heard Niki talking to Jax. "How far behind us are Scott and Mike? Did they stop for a late dinner and not invite us?"

"Call Scott's cell," Jax said.

She placed her phone on speaker as it rang. The sound vibrated inside Thomas's skull. With his senses at full alert, the ringing hurt. Finally, she ended the call.

"Can one of you help me with this gate?" Nate asked, still trying to muscle it open. "Unless you want to leave the cars here, and we walk everything in."

Two car doors opened as both Niki and Jax stepped out.

Thomas stayed on the far side of the car. He heard Nate struggle with the fence and could've opened it with ease, but something didn't feel right. The clanging of the fence filled his ears, making it hard to focus on anything besides that. He peered into the darkness; the moon gave off the only light. He stared deep into the shadows.

"Should we be worried about Scott and Mike?" Niki asked.

Closer than he liked, Thomas heard feet quickly hitting the pavement. With one leap, Thomas jumped on top of the car. That was when he heard his voice.

"I would be worried about them," came Silas's response.

Silas appeared out of the shadows along with six other vampires. Three stood to each side, flanking him. They approached where Jax, Niki, and Nate stood.

Thomas knew they were not only outnumbered, his friends were unarmed. Their typical weaponry for a raid was stashed inside Scott's and Mike's SUV. What little they had with them they kept stowed in hard shell containers in the back. They had no way to get to the armaments before Silas sicced his minions on them. Thomas could only think of one thing to do.

"Run!" he yelled to them.

Jax, Niki, and Nate sprinted through the small opening in the gate. They crossed the parking lot and ran up to the front door.

Thomas leapt down from the top of the SUV and stood between the gate and the seven vampires. He peered around at the assembled foe and was confident he could take them. They weren't fledglings, but they were young vampires. Probably a few weeks turned. They wore torn jeans, and shirts with blood splattered on them. They hadn't learned how to drink and not spill yet. Each had their arms clasped behind their back.

"Our fight isn't with you," Silas said. He turned to the three vampires on his right and pointed at two of them. "Move him."

The two brandished iron bars from behind their backs. Thomas took a step backward, losing a touch of his confidence, and they rushed at him. He blocked the first one's strike, but the second attacker hit him in the stomach.

Thomas doubled over, and a bar fell on his back. He kicked backward and sent one guy into the side of the SUV, denting the door and blowing out the windows. The other grabbed Thomas by the hair and hit him across the chest with the iron bar. Thomas fell to the ground, but still in front of the fence opening.

He glanced to the front of the building and saw Jax, Niki, and Nate close the door. He heard it latch. Thomas couldn't care less what happened to him, as long as they made it to safety.

Silas walked over to him and leaned into Thomas's face. "Stop being their savior and stay out of our way." He grabbed Thomas by the shirt, picked him up, and threw him onto the hood of the SUV. "We aren't here for you, brother. I can still forgive your betrayal."

Thomas, enraged at hearing Silas call him brother, hopped off of the hood of the car and hollered as he ran at Silas. His anger blinded him. Centuries of living with a brother who caused so much death and destruction flooded out of him, but it wasn't enough.

Silas caught Thomas by the neck and slammed him to the ground. "Enough!" he yelled at him. Silas marched to the front of the building and stood at the door. He grabbed the door handle and tugged a few times. Thomas started to smile, before Silas punched both hands into the steel door. Using his new hand holds, he broke the door off the hinges and tossed it aside. The six vampires, along with Silas, walked into Night Crew headquarters.

From beyond the fence, he could hear shelves being toppled, canisters broken, and supplies being destroyed. In their march of destruction, the six vampires threw anything they could find at the lights in the warehouse as if it was a game. Thomas heard them laughing each time a light shattered out of existence. He also heard Silas's taunts.

"Jax, my old friend. Where are you hiding? We will find you. Don't you worry that bald head of yours. I don't plan on turning you. Come out, come out, wherever you are."

I've got to stop them, *Thomas thought.* I'm not losing anyone else to him. *He stood and ran to the newly removed front door. Just as he stepped inside, he heard a gunshot. His friends had made it to the armory. He hoped they did, at least, and not that one of Silas's demons had fired that shot.*

Up ahead, he heard more smashing sounds. Shards of glass littered the walkway. All but one light remained, and it flickered, trying to stay alive. Their precious headquarters lay in ruins.

Thomas blamed himself. He knew Silas better than anyone. He should have known at some point Silas wasn't going to sit idly by and watch them continue to pick off his hives over and over. Eventually, Silas would go on the offensive and take the fight to them. Thomas had grown overconfident, caught up knowing they were getting closer to Silas. Silas hadn't run away this time but played him like a fiddle instead, and his associates were going to pay the price.

"Silas!" he yelled, going on the hunt within the building.

Thomas turned the corner into their makeshift meeting room. Surrounded by destroyed monitors, he saw a vampire with long hair hovering over Nate's body. He ran at the vampire and grabbed him by the back of the shirt. The vampire's eyes grew wide as Thomas caught him off guard. Thomas lifted the long-haired vampire off the ground and threw him into the wall. Thomas directed his hearing at Nate for a heartbeat. Finding one, he exhaled a sigh of relief.

The vampire hit the fencing with a crash, shattering another monitor and falling through the top of the desk to the ground. From a crouching position, Long Hair jumped at Thomas like a jaguar leaping at its intended prey.

Thomas grabbed Long Hair out of the air and slammed him into the large table the Night Crew sat around. He kept the struggling vampire pinned with one hand. He could definitely tell this vampire wasn't much beyond a fledgling and easily overpowered him. With his free arm, he grabbed Nate's machete off the floor next to Nate's unconscious body and forcibly swung it at the young vampire's neck. The head spun off to the side of the table, burying the machete's blade into the tabletop. Thomas flung the headless body to the side.

"Silas!" he screamed again. He turned down the hall to the break room. Glass from the fluorescent bulbs crunched beneath his feet. The security lights bathed the hallway in red.

Silas stepped into the hallway from the break room. "You hollered, brother?"

The two stood in the enclosed space only a few feet from each other.

"You are not my brother. His name was Benjamin, and you killed him."

"Oh Thomas, stop being so melodramatic," Silas said. "Benji just doesn't have that arch-villain, evil mastermind ring to it, does it? And from what I recall, I didn't kill me. You hold that honor. And on my wedding day, no less."

Silas stood there taunting Thomas, daring him to attack while the remaining vampires searched for Niki and Jax. It dawned on Thomas that Josh was also here somewhere, but he hadn't seen any sign of him.

"I remember very well," Thomas said, returning his attention to Silas. "I relive it in my nightmares. I try to atone for my sins."

"By hunting and killing your own kind? Oh, Thomas, you live such a lonely life. It would be so much easier if you didn't hate yourself. We are the alpha species. We sit on top of the food chain.

"I don't hate you for what you did. I embraced it, and now look at me." Silas outstretched his arms and placed each hand on an opposite wall in the small hallway. "Who needs religion when you have me? I'm god and savior. I give life through blood. I thank you for your gift, brother."

Thomas charged at Silas. His shoulder hit Silas in the stomach as Thomas tackled him. The two crashed into the break room. From across the hall, he heard more gunshots. Thomas pinned Silas to the floor and started punching him in the head.

Silas laughed while Thomas pummeled him. Thomas delivered shots to his head and to his side. The whole time, Silas continued to hold his arms outstretched, unfazed by Thomas's assault. After letting Thomas pound on him for a few moments, Silas clasped his hands together above his head, and with both fists, drove them into Thomas's chest, sending Thomas backward onto the floor and landing on his back.

"My turn," Silas said.

Silas, while lying on his back, pushed off the ground and landed on his feet. Thomas still lay sprawled on the floor. Silas stomped over and kicked him in the side. Then he reached down, grabbed Thomas by the shirt and picked him up. Thomas's coat dangled in the air around him. Silas slammed Thomas through a table and onto the ground. He picked Thomas up again and slammed him against the cabinets.

Thomas tried to reach for Silas, but Silas held Thomas by his throat. Silas grabbed a knife from the countertop and drove it through Thomas's left hand, burying it into the cabinet behind Thomas. He then grabbed another knife, sending it through Thomas's right hand, pinning him to the cabinets.

"You want to play martyr? Well, now you can look like their savior," Silas said, standing back up.

Thomas sat defeated on the floor. Unable to move his hands from the cabinet, he dropped his head. Blood fell from wounds on his chest, face, and hands.

"What are you trying to do?" he asked Silas, his head still bowed.

Silas walked a circle around the break room, then moved back in front of Thomas. He sat down in front of him and crossed his legs.

"Build an army, of course. We are on the top of the food chain. Why should our food dictate the rules to us?"

"You are going directly against the Accords," Thomas said.

"Fuck the Accords. They were made by weak members of a weak Council. With you and your Night Crew out of the way, I can finally finish. When I'm done, the Council will see the error of their ways. We'll be on top where we should be."

"What about the other members?" Thomas asked. His breathing became labored as blood continued to flow from his wounds. He was too weak to heal.

"I guess they'll just have to get onboard with the new management," he said. Footsteps sounded close to the door. "Well look what the cat dragged

in." Silas pointed as two of his vampires walked in. One had Jax thrown over his shoulder and the other had Niki. Both were bound and unconscious.

"Where are the others?" Silas asked.

"This guy killed two, and she took out Marion," the vampire holding Jax said. "I haven't seen Steven."

"If he's the one with the long hair, I gave him a haircut," Thomas said from the floor.

"I bring six and leave with two," Silas said.

"What are we doing with him?" the vampire holding Niki asked, pointing to Thomas.

"He's a lost cause. Find his blood bank and destroy it. He can either choose to starve to death or go back to being an animal."

Silas turned back to Thomas. "By the way, if you choose the latter, come visit. I'd love to have my old brother back by my side."

The two vampires dropped Jax and Niki on the ground and went to the back rooms. Thomas could hear them rummaging through the refrigerator. The smell of blood wafted in the air. In his head, Thomas saw all his blood supply covering the floor, spoiling.

"What are you going to do with them?" Thomas asked Silas.

"Oh, I'm going to take my time bleeding them. Killing them quickly would be too nice. I want them to make my army stronger. There's nothing sweeter than hunter blood. Well, besides young blood."

He paused and moved his finger in front of him like he was counting inventory. "Hey, where's your tech? That guy in the wheelchair?"

Thomas also wondered where Josh was. Every time they came back from a raid, Josh was here. He wouldn't have had time to escape anywhere without being seen. Thomas just shrugged at Silas.

"Hey, boys," Silas hollered. "When you're finished with the blood, there's still one person missing. A cripple. Shouldn't be too hard."

Thomas heard them move throughout the few remaining rooms in the warehouse. He heard bookshelves falling to the ground, and the ripping of bedsheets and mattresses. Did they think he was hiding in a mattress?

The two minions came back into the break room pushing Josh's wheelchair. "We found this but not him."

"And you searched everywhere?"

"Yeah," they said in unison.

"Fine. Pick up the three humans. I'm sure Jennings will have arrived by now with my treat. Yum yum." He looked back at Thomas. "Bye, brother."

Silas left out of the break room with the two vampires carrying Niki and Jax behind him. He heard them pick up Nate. Their footsteps crunched on broken glass as they walked out of the warehouse.

Thomas, pinned to the cabinet and helpless to stop Silas from taking his friends, screamed into the empty warehouse.

26

Thomas took his hand away from my temple. My head felt like a spike had been driven straight into the middle of it. A piercing pain radiated from between my eyes and wrapped the entirety of my skull.

"I'll give you a minute to recover," he told me.

I rubbed my head and my eyes. Damn that hurt. I massaged the back of my neck, trying to ease the tension that his mind meld caused.

I wanted vengeance for Brittany's death. That was why I joined the Night Crew. Now, instead of vengeance, my new friends were captured. They were going to slowly bleed to death, feeding the vampire army.

Did it just come down to Thomas and me to save the world? I thought I gave up world saving when I left the military.

I let my head fall backward against the cabinet, resting it there with my eyes closed.

I can't do this, Brit.

Yes, you can, she whispered inside my head. *They need you.*

I'm not strong enough.

Stop doubting yourself. You are stronger than you know.

I saw what he did to Thomas. How do I stop someone that powerful?

Because you always rise to the occasion, Brittany said.

The sound of her voice always calmed me. Although I only knew her for a few years, a short time in the grand scheme of things, she was my rock through so much. I never would've made it through my parents' deaths if not for her. God knows where I would be, but I doubt it would be here.

I took a deep breath in. Slowly, I opened my eyes and stared at Thomas still sitting next to me.

"Jax never mentioned that ability during training," I told him.

"We don't use it much. Too often and it could kill you."

Feeling the throb within my head, I believed him.

"You can't imagine the number of questions I have, right now," I said. "First on the list, though... What happened to Josh?"

"Oh yes," Thomas said. "My guess is he's in the back storage closet, probably above the ceiling tiles. Now that I've regained some of my strength, I can help him down. I have you to thank for that."

"Above the ceiling tiles in the storage closet?" I reiterated, hopping to my feet. The arm wrapped with my shirt felt sore from the puncture wounds. My head swam briefly from the sudden elevation change and lack of blood. I caught myself against the cabinets and steadied.

Thomas stood up, his coat stopping mid-thigh and his shirt still torn. The slashes on his chest had already begun to heal over. His hands stopped bleeding, and the stigmata-like wounds faded to barely notice-able. He strode out of the break room and stopped just outside of the storage closet door.

The red security lights bathed the walls in a blood-like glow. I left out after Thomas and stepped in front of him. He just stood there. I thought it odd that he wasn't walking further to help. "Something wrong?"

"This is about as close as I can get," he said. "You'll have to help him."

"Josh!" I screamed down the hallway. "Josh, it's Thomas and Mike."

"Thank God," came a muffled voice from the end of the hallway. "Glad to hear your voice. You mind giving me a hand."

"On the way," I cried back. I turned to Thomas. "You aren't helping?"

"I can't go any further. Too pungent," he said. He took a few steps backward, the glass crunching under his boots as he did.

I hurried to the end of the hallway and opened the storage closet door. The closet was small with a basin in the corner, a mop bucket, and a broom. A few cleaning supplies sat on the shelf. On the floor, pieces of a shattered ceiling tile lay scattered. Up above, Josh's head poked through the ceiling.

"Thomas," I said and glanced down the hallway. He had moved out of sight.

"He's not going to help," Josh said. "He can't."

"He said the same thing. Why not?"

"Garlic," he answered.

"Garlic?" I asked. I took a deep whiff of the air. I did smell a slight hint of garlic but dismissed it from our lunch earlier that day.

"From the cameras, I saw what happened outside," he said. As he spoke, he shifted his legs into the hole in the ceiling. He started to lower himself, and I stood underneath, helping to guide him down. "I grabbed the syringe of garlic extract and injected myself. I grabbed another syringe and sped down the hallway to this closet. I poured the garlic extract directly onto the floor and the door, hoisted myself up here, and slid the tile back in place."

I listened in disbelief at the quick thinking. Once Josh was out of the ceiling, I helped him onto the floor. His wheelchair lay thrown down the hall, and I went to get it. "So they couldn't find you because of the smell?" I started back with the wheelchair.

"I heard those two idiots, but they never touched the door, let alone opened it," Josh said. "I'm guessing similar to Thomas not being able to come down the hallway. That much pure garlic, and they couldn't get close."

Josh hopped into the chair and wheeled his way to the break room. Thomas sat at the back of the room. Josh stared at him. "You look like shit."

"You can say that," Thomas replied and glanced over at me. I read the thank you in his eyes.

"How did you know where he was?" I asked Thomas.

"The smell of garlic from the hallway has been growing stronger and stronger. We don't keep garlic in the wash closet. I knew it must've been something he did. Ceiling tiles were a guess."

I picked up a table that wasn't destroyed and arranged a few chairs. Josh slid up to it, and Thomas and I sat down. "We need to save the others," I said.

"How do you expect we do that?" Josh asked. "Are they even still alive?"

Thomas and I filled Josh in on what Silas said.

"Where are they keeping them?" he asked.

"I may have the answer to that," I said. "Thomas, I'll need your help. Follow me."

27

Thomas and I stood by the trunk of my Acura while Josh stayed inside the warehouse taking inventory of what wasn't damaged. That seemed to be a smaller list than what was. The night air tasted stale, like a closed room in an old house. The moon offered the only light. The street had one streetlight with a broken bulb, and Josh said they kept the one by the warehouse turned off purposefully.

"He was pretty talkative earlier when I was the one handcuffed in the backseat. Think he'll be equally as talkative now?" I asked Thomas.

"He'll talk," he said confidently. His eyes glowed red, piercing the darkness.

Images of the floating red eyes from my childhood, that misplaced memory, drifted back to the surface. My ears rang with Martin's scream for help. It echoed in my head.

I closed my eyes for a moment and shook the thought away.

"Are you ok?" Thomas asked.

"Yeah," I said, not sure if I was lying or not. "Bad memory that keeps popping back up."

"Nightmares are something I'm very familiar with."

I held the key fob in my hand. "Let's say hi, shall we?" With a click of the button, the trunk lid hinged open, and the interior light came to life.

Detective Jennings lay curled up inside the trunk with his arms bent behind his back. Bleeding red marks encircled his wrists where the handcuffs were positioned. His eyes dilated, and he blinked to gain his focus. He immediately started to flail in the trunk like a fish out of water, hoping to throw himself out.

"You're a dead man, White," he yelled. "Dead. I don't care what Silas wants to do with you, I'm going to kill you myself."

I held out my hand toward Thomas, and Thomas handed me the duct tape. I pulled a few inches free from the roll and leaned in, reaching for Jennings' head.

He stopped flailing to get out and started to scoot backward away from me. "Do not put that on me," he shouted.

"Thomas, a hand please," I calmly said.

Thomas reached around me and grabbed Jennings by the shoulders. He pulled the overweight detective forward with ease. As fast as Thomas pulled him, the carpet had to leave burns on his arm.

The sudden movement left the detective momentarily stunned. It gave me enough time to place the duct tape on his mouth. I wrapped it around his head twice, leaving enough room for his nose. No reason to suffocate him in the back of my car.

Jennings began struggling again as I tore the duct tape off the roll. His eyes bulged from his head, but they still harbored defiance in them. He quickly and audibly puffed air in and out of his nose.

I leaned my head into the trunk, stopped a few inches from his face, and stared directly into his eyes. "Now that I have your attention," I told him, "we're going to go inside and have a little conversation. How well you cooperate determines the number of pieces you make it home in. Am I clear? Nod if so."

Jennings, eyes still bulging out of their sockets and fuming with rage, heavily breathing through his nose, quickly nodded in agreement.

"Good. Now for the first test of your cooperation. Behave for my friend."

I pulled my head out of the trunk and stepped away. Thomas took my place and bent over the opening. He reached in, grasped Jennings by the shoulders again, and hoisted the detective onto his shoulder.

Jennings' arms and back faced the night sky. His feet kept straight as a board in front of Thomas. His head fell midway down Thomas's back.

Thomas led the way back through the broken door, and I followed behind him. Josh rummaged through a case on the floor, counting its contents and notating them on his tablet. Thomas and I turned past our meeting area with the headless vampire still lying there, down the hallway only lit by the red security light, and into the break room. As Thomas turned into the break room, he angled toward the wall and harshly sat Detective Jennings on the floor next to it. When his butt hit the linoleum, the air quickly left Jennings' lungs.

I came in after Thomas and marched straight to an overturned table—one of the few left intact. I sat the round table upright and placed two chairs on opposite sides of it. I motioned for the detective to come join me, and I sat. Thomas hovered by the cabinets, close to where he was pinned not that long ago.

Jennings placed his feet underneath him and used the wall to worm his way up. When he stood fully erect, he stretched his back and shoulders. He was still dressed in his stereotypical detective uniform of a white button shirt and blue dress slacks. The shirt was now partially torn and missing a few buttons. Burgundy blood stains randomly dotted the upper portion of his shirt. Dried blood colored his face around his cheeks and eyes like grotesque makeup.

He popped his neck and marched over to the chair. With his foot, he kicked the chair out from the table. He stared at me without sitting.

"Is there a problem, Officer?" I teased.

He bobbed his shoulders up and down. He also motioned his head toward his handcuffed hands. I understood the message and tossed Thomas the keys to the cuffs.

Thomas caught them in the air and moved to the detective. The key fumbled around the handcuffs. Finally, Jennings brought his free hands in front of his body as Thomas resumed his position.

He rolled his wrists to stretch them out and sat at the table. He took a deep breath, raised his arms to his face, and quickly unraveled the duct tape from his head. With his mouth free, he stretched out his jaw. The duct tape contained scabs of dried blood, and cuts around Jennings' mouth began to produce red pearls of fresh blood.

"Feel better?" I asked.

"That's much better," he said.

"Good to hear. Now, where did they take my friends?" I went straight to the point instead of screwing around with niceties.

"How about fuck you and your blood sucker? He's going to kill each and every one of you, and I'm going to smile and laugh while he does. I hope he guts you from throat to testicles while you're still alive to feel it," he shouted. He placed his hands on the table in front him.

I leaned forward in my chair, placing my hands in my lap. "Interesting but wrong answer. This will be your last warning, though. Each time after this, there will be a punishment."

"Fuck you!" he screamed at me.

"Sorry," I said. "You aren't my type." I stayed leaning forward in my chair with my hands in my lap.

He leaned forward, arms on the table. "I'm sure. Your type is dead red heads."

With that, I quickly brought my arm from under the table. My hand held one of the kitchen knives Silas drove through Thomas's hands. Like Silas did to Thomas, I buried the blade into Jennings' hand and through the table. The knife didn't stop until the hilt touched the top of his hand.

The detective screamed in pain while my hand continued to grasp the knife's handle. He recoiled so violently, the chair shot out from under him. His knees hit the floor, and his arm stayed suspended across the top of the table.

I grasped the hilt tighter and slowly applied a slight amount of torque. "When did you start working for Silas?" I yelled at him over cries. "When?"

He raised his head just enough so that his eyes cleared the top of the table, while I leaned in closer, his stuck hand just under my chest. I applied more downward pressure and torque before letting up.

Through clenched teeth, he finally choked out, "About a month ago."

"So you've offered fellow citizens...children...who you are supposed to serve and protect... up to Silas like lambs to the slaughter?" I slowly twisted the blade, feeling it grind against a bone in his hand. Droplets of blood dripped through the table onto the floor. "For a month, the only person you've served has been Silas?"

"Yes," he yelled out in guttural pain. "Yes, goddammit!"

"Where? Where are they? Where is Silas keeping Jax, Niki, and Nate?" This time, I pressed down on the hilt of the knife instead of turning. I'd found switching back and forth to be an effective means of getting information.

"If I tell you, I'm a dead man," he cried.

I peered up at Thomas who had a smile on his face. He enjoyed watching the detective squirm. The ass kicking by Silas must've awakened his thirst for vengeance as well.

"If you don't tell me, you're a dead man, and we've already caught you," I told him. "I'll at least let you live. What you do after you leave here is up to you." I eased the pressure I put on the knife in his hand. "Where are they?"

"The club," he said.

"The club?" I asked. "You mean Club Starlight?"

"Yes." His breathing slowed. The pain must've abated since I stopped adding more pressure. The blood loss probably helped to numb his hand.

In my head, I thought back to when I sat handcuffed in the back of my car. "Think of them as being on tap," he'd said while I figured out how to escape. He gave a smart-ass answer telling me exactly where they'd be. What an asshole!

"Is that Silas's base of operation?" Thomas asked, still standing by the cabinets.

"That's where he does all his business, if that's what you mean," Jennings said.

"Is that where he sleeps?" Thomas asked.

"No," he said.

I gripped the knife hard and slightly turned it. He let out a sharp cry as the pain surged through his hand.

"I'm telling the truth," he shouted. "He doesn't stay there."

"Where does he stay?" I asked directly.

"I don't know," he cried back from under the table. After adding more pressure to the knife, he said, "I promise, I don't know. No one does."

"That sounds like Silas," Thomas said, glancing at me. "Keeps himself safe by not telling anyone. He lets his lieutenants, the betas, and the fledglings fend for themselves while he stays safely hidden away. We keep exterminating the nests but never killing the queen, so to speak."

"We know he's been building an army," I said, leaning further over the table so Jennings knew I was talking to him. "We know he plans on keeping our friends on tap as you put it." I gave a quick turn of the blade as I said it. "When is he putting his plan into action?"

"Tomorrow night," he yelled through tears. "Tomorrow night at the club. According to Silas, he's going to have a recruitment party."

I looked at Thomas and mouthed the words "Recruitment party?"

His face immediately told me my answer. "Not good," he finally said.

"Anything else we need from him?" I asked Thomas.

"Not right now," he responded.

Leaning back in the chair, I pulled the knife from Jennings' hand. He immediately dropped it down below the table where he sat. Thomas tossed him a hand towel, and Jennings quickly wrapped his hand with it. Two small maroon dots started expanding on the white towel from the top and bottom of his hand.

"What would you like to do with him, now?" Thomas asked, pointing to the wounded man under the table.

Jennings used his legs to scoot to the pole at the center of the table, cowering away from Thomas.

"For starters, let's do some first aid on his hand. No reason we can't show compassion, even though he is a disgrace and a piece of shit. Then, toss him back into the trunk." I heard Jennings whimper from under the table. I kept talking to Thomas. "I said we wouldn't kill him, and I plan to keep my word. It's up to him if he wants to avoid Silas and hide or run back to him begging for his forgiveness."

Thomas looked somewhat disappointed. "Michael, you are a better man than I."

"Thank you," I responded, flattered by the compliment. "I need to speak with Josh. Do you mind doctoring him up?"

Thomas gave a nod.

I pushed my chair back from the table and bent down toward the detective. The towel wrapped around his hand had two sizable red blotches on it. "Behave for Thomas. If you do, you'll stay alive. You have my word. If you don't, I can't guarantee your head won't be on backward."

With that, I stood and left the break room. Sweat had formed on my brow, and I wiped it off as I ventured down the hallway still bathed in red light. From behind me, I heard the water in the sink begin to run. *Please don't kill him, Thomas.*

28

In the warehouse, Josh continued to take inventory. He sat underneath a shelf that leaned against the wall. Boxes lay at his feet.

"How bad?" I asked.

"Could've been worse," he said. He wheeled out from underneath a shelf that now looked more like a lean-to. "They didn't set off any of the silver grenades, so we have a ton of those. Mainly destroyed a lot of office supplies and toiletries. They ran through here so fast, they didn't destroy the armory, only scattered things." He pointed to the corner he was working in. "Silver-jacket bullets are under there next to the grenades. Still have a few machetes there as well. Couple of the shotguns are broken in half, but others are fine. All in all, I've seen worse."

"That's not nearly as bad as I thought," I said. "I'm guessing you haven't talked to Intel since all this happened, right?"

"No, not yet."

I filled Josh in on what Detective Jennings told Thomas and me. "I think we should get Intel on the line and fill them in. See what kind of help we can get for a rescue operation."

Josh started to roll toward the meeting area. "I'll get them online. You know, Mike, you keep going like this, and you'll be running your own crew soon."

"I'm just here to kill Silas, remember? Then I am going back to my old life and figuring out how to live without Brittany."

"I've heard that said before," Josh said smiling.

"Just get them on the horn," I shot back.

Josh continued on to what was left of our meeting area.

I lingered behind him, turning toward the mess he'd inventoried. The single light bulb cast shadows all around. Fortunately, it decided to stay lit and stopped flickering like a strobe light.

When I placed my hand on the shelving unit that leaned against the wall, it shifted awkwardly. I bent low and crawled underneath it. Since the contents of the shelves lay scattered on the floor, I decided to grasp the whole thing in my hands and push it back up. It rocked on its legs and almost tipped the other direction before I steadied it. I knew cleaning this place up would have to be a team effort but might as well make little fixes where I could. That made it a lot easier to see the contents on the ground.

From behind me, I heard the sound of shuffling and the hard footfalls of boots on concrete. I turned around and saw Thomas marching Jennings my direction. Thomas still wore his coat and ripped up white shirt. His steps echoed through the warehouse.

A few feet in front of Thomas, Detective Jennings dragged his feet, making the walk to the car excruciatingly slow. I could only imagine how annoyed Thomas had become. The bloody towel had been replaced by gauze, wrapped in ice, and all held together by duct tape. He held it at chest level as they headed for the door.

"Hey Thomas," I said. "Keep an eye on him for now. Josh is dialing up Intel for me. After my conversation with them, we can take care of our friend."

"I'm not a babysitter," he said dejectedly.

"It won't take long. Also," I raised my voice to make sure Jennings heard, "if he does anything other than sit in the car waiting like a good boy, break the wrist of his other hand. He'll have plenty of time to think about his poor decisions since he won't be able to play with himself."

Jennings turned around at the door, glaring at me. "Silas is going to come for you, and he's going to kill you. If I'm not dead by then, I'm going to laugh while he does it."

"Good to know," I said. "Don't mouth off to Thomas while you two wait for me. He isn't as kind natured as I am."

Thomas shook his head at me and lumbered out of the front door just behind the detective.

"Mike," Josh hollered from the meeting area. "Mike, I found a working laptop. Dialing up Intel now."

I jogged over to the meeting area. The machete was still buried in the table like Excalibur stuck in the stone. It took a dozen tugs before I freed it. Thomas had swung it with such incredible force, I was surprised he hadn't split the table in two.

With the machete free, I strode over to the headless vampire corpse on the floor while Josh sat at the table with the laptop in front of him. I grabbed an arm and dragged the body to the middle of the warehouse. The sound of ringing filled the open space.

After several rings, I heard a click. "Intel here."

The vampire's arm dropped out of my hand, and I froze. I knew I didn't hear that right. It couldn't have been. Shaking my head, I reached back down to grab the arm again.

"Intel, Josh here. We've had an incident and need assistance."

"What happened, Josh?"

I dropped the arm a second time and yelled, "No fucking way."

29

I marched back toward the meeting area and went around the table toward Josh and the laptop. "Hey, you son of a bitch, how do you stop a Syrian tank?" I grabbed the top of the laptop and spun it toward me.

Austin Jeffries filled the laptop screen. He still wore his brown hair in a military buzz cut. Glasses sat on his nose above a square jawline accented with a goatee.

"You shoot the guy pushing it, of course," came the reply. "How've you been, Mike?"

I rubbed my temples and my eyes in disbelief. Austin, the army grunt turned military intelligence that once upon a time we left handcuffed to a flagpole because he said he watched a video on how to escape, answered the call Josh made to Intel. I stood up straight and took a few steps backward. "Unbelievable!" was the only word I could say, and I said it a few times.

Josh sat back, confused, with his eyes bouncing from the laptop screen to me and back again.

"Mike," Austin said. "Mike, I'm sure you have a ton of questions, right now."

I turned to the laptop and leaned into the camera, staring at him. My eyes swelled up with tears that streamed down my face. I stared into his eyes. "Only one. I only have one *fucking* question, right now. When you called me the other day...did you know? Did you know who killed her?"

I balled up my hands into fists and I pressed them into my eyes, forcing the tears down my cheeks.

"Mike, it's not that..." he started.

"*Answer the fucking question*!" I yelled into the laptop screen. Spittle flew from my lips as I screamed at him.

"Yes, I knew it was Silas," Austin said.

I felt betrayed by my best friend. In Afghanistan, I saved his ass more times than I could count. We were brothers. He knew who'd killed Brittany. He'd called me acting shocked. He even recommended I use my gift to investigate on my own. And for what? To flush Silas out because Austin and the Night Crew couldn't find him themselves?

In that moment, I felt like bait. They used the opportunity of my wife's murder to make me bait. Why not turn a tragedy into a good thing? Camp Anger doesn't explain it. I napalmed Camp Anger and turned it into Camp Nitro Infused Fucking Nuclear Anger.

Suddenly, I felt sick. With my hands behind my head, I took a few steps away from the screen, squatted, and fell backward onto the concrete floor. I took slow deep breaths in and out.

"Josh," I heard Austin say. "Give him a minute."

Josh's eyes never left me. The whole warehouse fell silent. I heard my breath and my heartbeat pulse inside my head. Wrapped in the silence of the room, I focused on my breathing. Focused on regaining my sense of control and calmness.

Focus on the mission, I told myself. *Silas. Silas was my mission. Kill Silas, then go back to life after Brittany.* I had to look beyond the feeling of betrayal. There'd be time for that later. For now, I had a mission. I pushed my emotions down into my stomach and focused on that mission.

My breathing slowed, and my body began to relax. I dropped my hands and unclenched my fists, willing my muscles to release their tension. I placed them on the ground, moved my legs under my body, and stood back up. With my bloodshot eyes open, I leaned my head back, took a deep breath in, and audibly exhaled turning back to the monitor.

I grabbed a chair that sat at the table in front of me, pulled it back, and sat. Josh adjusted the laptop toward me.

"Nice to have you back, Sergeant," Austin said.

"Austin, we have a lot of catching up to do. Next time you're in Texas, you owe me a beer right after I give you a black eye."

"Looking forward to it," he said. He genuinely smiled, and I reciprocated just not as genuinely.

"Silas and some of his betas took Jax, Nate, and Niki. They trashed the headquarters and almost killed Thomas."

"Straight to business, I see. I know you and Josh are alive. What about Scott?"

"Dead as far as I know," I told him. "He and I were jumped at the farmhouse. That detective I told you about, Jennings, he's working for Silas. He captured me earlier and told me Scott was dead."

"One second," he said. He made a few movements with his hand and looked away from the camera. He began typing. "That's Detective John Jennings, correct?"

"Yeah," I answered.

"Obviously you escaped. Is he dead, and, if so, where's the body?"

"No, he's alive. I interrogated him."

Austin's eyes turned toward the camera again as if he was looking straight at me. "*You* interrogated him?" he asked.

"Not my first time, you know."

"Oh, I'm aware," he said. "How bad of shape is he in?"

"Thomas patched him up, but that's not what's important. Back on task, grunt."

"You do know you're retired, and I actually hold a higher rank now. I'll let it slide this time, Sergeant," he said, trying to sound official.

"Did I re-enlist and not realize it?" I asked.

"Hell no. This is way better," he said with a smile. "Alright back on track. Let me make sure I have this right. Silas has Jax, Niki, and Nate. You're sure they're still alive?"

"Yes," I answered. "The arrogant bastard wants to slowly bleed them to feed his army. They're being held at Club Starlight."

"Club Starlight. Got it. And you said army? What do you mean?"

"I mean according to him, he's tired of his food making the rules. He mentioned something about the Accords and the Council," I said. I closed my eyes, taking myself back through Thomas's vision. "'Weak members of a weak Council' is what he told Thomas."

"The Council will not be happy with him," Austin said. He shook his head as he spoke "They've worked hard to keep the peace. We've known Silas was an outlier, but, according to you, he's staging a revolution. In the eyes of the Council, that's treason."

"Who is the Council and what are the Accords?" I finally asked. Those questions had been bouncing in my head since I'd first heard about them. Based on the context, though, I had an idea.

"Have Josh or Thomas fill you in. For now, what else don't I know?" Austin asked.

"He's having a recruitment party tomorrow night, and the Night Crew is the main course. What's a recruitment party?" I asked.

"You don't want to know," he avoided answering. "Tomorrow night? That doesn't leave much time for recon or planning."

"Austin, tell me this, do you work for Intel, or are you Intel?"

He raised one side of his mouth in a smirk. "Right now, what's the difference?"

"Good point," I said. I sat back in my chair, staring at my old friend on the screen typing furiously. "Where do we go from here?"

"It's a little after midnight there, right?" he asked, and I nodded in reply. "Get some rest if you can. By late morning, I'll have information for you."

"Thanks, Austin."

"And Mike," he said as I reached for the laptop to spin it toward Josh. "I'm sorry I didn't tell you before. If I knew he was coming after her..." he started but trailed off, shaking his head. His eyes became bloodshot holding back tears. "I love you like a brother," he finally said.

"Mutual. Now, let's get our team back," I told him and turned the laptop toward Josh. My back rested against the back of the chair. I gazed up at the rafters above us as I set there.

"Thanks, Austin, I mean Intel," Josh said. "I'll await your direction."

The laptop made a noise indicating the connection hung up. When Josh lowered the lid, it clicked shut. "You okay?" he asked me.

"Not at all. Like Austin said, though, get some rest, if you can. Thomas and I need to make a delivery before this night's over for me. I have a feeling tomorrow night is going to be equally long."

I stood from the chair, pushed it under the table, and headed toward the front door.

30

Walking out of the building, I saw Jennings sitting in the backseat of my car, duct tape stretched across his mouth. Handcuffs kept his arms fastened behind his back. His hair stuck to his head from a combination of sweat and dried blood. His head rested against the window.

Thomas sat comfortably in the passenger seat in front of him. He looked relaxed with his eyes closed, waiting for me to join.

I opened the driver's side door and sat behind the steering wheel.

Without opening his eyes, Thomas asked, "Where are we taking your friend?"

"I know a good place," I said as I put the car in gear. "Did he give you any trouble?"

"No, but I didn't want to hear anything in case he felt like speaking."

"Works for me."

I peeled out of the parking lot, back onto the darkened road in front of the warehouse, until it joined with the highway.

The detective sat silent in the backseat; his head stayed against the door. I assumed he contemplated what was in store for him next. Would I stay true to my word of not killing him? Or was I taking him out to pasture? I also imagined he was terrified of what Silas would do to him once Silas found him. Jennings' simple task of bringing me to his boss went incredibly wrong. I had no doubt Jennings feared for his life on both fronts.

As we drove down the empty highway, I decided to broach a conversation with Thomas. "Story time," I said. "Tell me about the Accords."

Thomas, who had remained slouched in the passenger seat with his eyes closed, slowly opened them and sat up in his seat. "What do you want to know about them?"

"Everything. What are they? When did they start? What's the Council?"

"So from the beginning, then?" he asked.

"From the beginning."

Thomas took a deep breath. "Both the Council and the Accords came into existence centuries before I was born. What I know, I learned from talking to those older than me. Supposedly, the Council has a historian, and the records go back to the beginning of the Council's creation. I've never seen them, and I've never met anyone who has. Just rumors."

"Do they have a name or does everyone just call them 'The Council'?" I made air quotes around the term.

Thomas smiled. "Just the Council."

"How far back does this go?"

"The Dark Ages. Before that, the Roman Empire held enough strength to keep people protected from the shadows. But when their empire finally fell, a darkness enveloped the known world. Villages had to fend for themselves, and most didn't have the knowledge or resources to be able to. People tried to hide in the shadows, but so did the creatures of the night.

"A war broke out between families and kinds."

"Families and kinds?" I asked.

"By kinds I mean between vampires, werewolves, banshees, witches, ankous, baykoks, and other things your nightmares can't imagine. Some were completely exterminated. Others descended into different regions of the world similar to an exile."

"What did they fight over?"

"Food, of course," Thomas said. "Humans. They fought over who could control the food source, and who could be turned to create more creatures. Even within the various kinds, families fought. Within vampires, for instance, an Alpha would claim his herd. If another Alpha encroached on his territory, there would be a bloody fight until only one remained. There existed a constant struggle between wanting to eat, wanting to create more, and not extinguishing their food supply."

"People were cattle," I commented out loud.

"Yes, those who couldn't fight or didn't have someone to fight for them were cattle."

"What changed?"

"Charlemagne," he said.

"Charlemagne?" I asked. "Like Charles the Great, the first of the Holy Roman Emperors?"

"Yes, that one. There's a reason he's been called the Father of Europe. During his rise to power, he knew he could never build his empire with the way things were. He amassed an army of soldiers, an elite force, trained in battling creatures of all kinds; the first Night Crew. Except, this was a whole army, and he began a total creature annihilation in the lands he controlled."

"If he went all through Europe liberating people, how are there still vampires and the rest?"

"He didn't have to go through all of Europe. For that matter, he didn't want to kill them all. Charlemagne knew a controlled population would have its benefits. After demonstrating his power, showing them what he could do, he summoned the heads of all the families to a meeting. Knowing the force he controlled, he convinced them of a way to coexist."

I nodded realizing where Thomas was headed. "The Council and the Accords."

"Correct," he said. "With the threat of extinction being held over them, each kind elected members to the Council. Charlemagne sat at the head of the Council, always maintaining control with the threat of extermination. The Council laid out the rules of order, or rules of engagement, you can also say. These became the Accords, and they've remained nearly intact since their inception."

"All the centuries since then, since Charlemagne's army has long passed, and they haven't simply decided to toss them in the trash?"

"Some have tried. There've been uprisings like what Silas wants to do, but cooler heads prevailed. Plus, although that army doesn't exist, there is still an enforcement arm to the Accords."

"The Night Crew?" I asked.

"The Night Crew is Jax's name, but yes."

"If there are others besides just us, why does Silas think he can bring about a revolution? Won't the Council send another group to quell whatever he wants to start?"

Thomas contemplated the answer. Finally, he said, "I don't know. What he's doing has been tried before and failed. I don't know why he thinks he's special. Granted, the bastard has always been privileged. Even in our youth, when he was my brother Benjamin and not this monster, he felt he was above everyone else.

"We weren't part of the elite growing up, but we didn't go hungry. Our parents made sure we were well taken care of. Benjamin, though, always desired more. He wanted to be part of the delegation in Philadelphia and was personally offended when he wasn't selected."

Thomas paused a moment, getting lost in the memory. I knew the look well. "I digress," he said, bringing himself back to the present.

"Hey, Detective," I yelled into the backseat.

Jennings raised his head from the door.

"We're almost there. Has Thomas's history lesson been putting you to sleep?"

In the rear-view mirror, I saw him roll his eyes and go back to staring out the window. In the darkness, trees rushed past on both sides. The town sat five miles behind us.

"What's in the Accords?" I asked Thomas.

"First off, the Accords created boundaries for each family. To end the infighting, the Council knew different groups needed to be separated. That was the first step.

"After creating boundaries, the Council established the rules of engagement. These were at the heart of the Accords. It regulated how many humans could be turned. How many vampires could be created, for instance. The goal was to not eliminate their food source. Find non-lethal or alternative ways of feeding."

"Alternative ways of feeding?"

Thomas gave a little chuckle. "This was how blood banks started. A reservoir of food donated by people. It was much simpler to donate blood for drinking later instead of being hunted like prey at night.

"With all of that, a police force was established to help control any rogue members."

"Such as Silas," I said.

"Exactly," he responded. "Just like Silas. This police force acts on orders from the Council. The person Josh called Intel is our liaison to the Council. The majority of governments around the world work with the Council. If the Accords dissolve, if the Council is uprooted like Silas wants, and everything goes back to anarchy, it would be a blood bath. Another Dark Ages could spring up."

"I don't think Silas wants anarchy. I think he wants to be crowned king."

I noticed the highway signs and slowed the car. The detective perked up in the backseat, and swiveled his head from one side to another as if trying to figure out where I had driven to. I killed the headlights, pulled onto the shoulder, and turned down a small dirt road off the highway.

"What is this place?" Thomas asked.

"When I was in high school, we used to come out here to drink and make out."

"And we are going to leave him here?"

"Of course."

I put the car in park, opened the driver's side door, and stepped into the night air. The area was just as I remembered it those years ago. Trees lined the small gravel road. A small farmhouse sat about three quarters of a mile further down. Broken beer bottles and condom wrappers littered the grass.

Thomas exited from the passenger side. He stood up and stretched his arms to the sky. In the shadows, his just over six-foot stature seemed to extend unnaturally far. Thomas opened the rear door and pulled Jennings from the back.

"One last thing," I said moving to the two of them, but speaking directly to our captive. "You ambushed me and my friend, and assuming you aren't lying about Scott, he didn't deserve to be killed without a fighting chance." My anger started to build in my throat. The image of Scott on the ground being dragged away appeared in my vision. My voice quivered holding back my rage. "Just because your boss wants me for some reason, didn't mean he needed to die."

Jennings stood still listening to me talk while Thomas held a firm grip on his arm.

From my back pocket, I pulled out my pocketknife. Jennings recoiled when he saw it and stiffened. His body told him to run, but Thomas's hand clamped down tighter.

"I'm not going to kill you," I continued. "I made you a promise that I wouldn't as long as you told me what I needed to know. I don't break my promises. As my wife lay dying in my arms, I promised her I would kill the bastard who hurt her, and I still plan to. I'm going to end Silas and the revolution he wants to start. I didn't ask to be a part of this, and

I don't intend to be a part of it any longer than I have to be. You killed my friend and tried to make me break my promise to my wife. I'm not going to kill you," I repeated to him.

"Thomas, hold him tight. Don't let him move."

Thomas gripped Jennings' shoulder using both hands. With his arms still handcuffed behind him and his mouth duct taped, he didn't have much struggle left in him.

I raised my pocketknife in front of his face, touched his chin with the flat of the steel blade, and moved it down to the top of his shirt. I used the knife to remove the buttons, then pulled the garment behind his back until it stopped at the handcuffs. I nodded to Thomas, and he grabbed the shirt, ripping it completely off.

Jennings recoiled at the pain in his shoulders and his injured hand.

Bringing the knife back in front of Jennings, I sliced his undershirt in half starting at the neckline and moving all the way down. Thomas finished off the shirt with a quick tug past the cuffs.

Jennings stood shirtless. His rotund stomach and chest heaved with every long, controlled breath through his nose.

"Thomas, can you place him on the ground, please?" I said calmly enough to sound frighteningly eerie.

With a quick motion, Thomas swept Jennings' legs out from under him, and he fell hard to the ground.

"Remove his shoes, pants, and underwear. Hopefully he hasn't shit himself."

For the first time since leaving headquarters, the detective started to struggle. While on the ground, his eyes grew wide, and he started to frantically kick in the air. Even as Thomas grabbed one leg to rip off a shoe, Jennings continued to kick with the other.

Unfortunately for him, though, Thomas didn't seem to care. Thomas grabbed the first foot, ripped the shoe off, and threw it into the trees. He repeated with the second one. Then, Thomas grabbed the cuffs of

Jennings' pants, and with one quick motion, his pants disappeared. His underwear traveled to his knees when he lost his pants, making them easy to remove.

"Now stand up," I told Detective Jennings.

Jennings scurried across the ground on his naked ass, kicking with his feet. When he felt like he wasn't in arm's reach anymore, he maneuvered himself to his knees and stood up.

"The town is about seven miles that way. If you survive the trip back, you will not survive the next time I see you."

I turned and sauntered back to the car. Thomas stood to my right. When I glanced over at him, a smirk spread across his face. We both opened our respective doors and sat inside.

"I saw that smile, Mr. Price," I told him with a grin of my own.

"Instead of killing him, you left him naked and handcuffed with duct tape across his face. Plus a seven mile walk in the middle of the night. Where did you learn that from?"

"So Austin, the guy who Josh calls Intel, well, he and I were in Afghanistan together. Austin used to tell us a story about this guy his sister dated who supposedly cheated on her. Austin and his buddies couldn't exactly kill him, but they sure as hell made him wish he was dead. They did something similar to that guy, except it was the beginning of the summer, and they covered him with honey. According to Austin, he was covered in flies, gnats, and ants by the time he finally made it back to town. The guy never said a word about who did it, and Austin's sister never heard from him again."

"Effective," Thomas said.

"Very," I agreed.

With the car in gear, I punched the gas, sending up dust and gravel around the naked man on the dirt road. I lost sight of him in the cloud of dust.

31

Thomas and I sat in silence as I drove back into town. With his eyes closed, he appeared to be resting. Although unless the earlier fight with Silas still weighed on him, I doubted he actually was. A few times, I almost interrupted the silence to ask him, but instead I left him alone.

The drone of the road sent me into my own thoughts.

The images of holding Brittany still haunted me. Despite everything I've seen since, I kept being drawn back to that moment. She lay cradled in my lap. The beating of her heart betrayed her. Instead of pumping blood through her body, it sent her blood gushing onto the rug and the carpet by way of her neck and chest wounds.

The sound of her drowning accompanied the images. Damn my brain and the vividness of my memories! I heard her drowning, trying to breathe. Her lungs begged for air but only filled with her own blood. The little air she grasped bubbled out of her, but not from her mouth. The sound escaped from her chest. Openings created where openings shouldn't be.

I brought my left hand to my face while my right remained on the steering wheel. I quickly rubbed the building tears out of my eyes and brought my hand down to my mouth, my neck, and finally rested it back in my lap.

My thoughts needed to stay on the task at hand and not drift away. I could work my way back through the stages of grief, back to Camp Acceptance, when I remove Silas's head from his shoulders.

I could hear the counselor from so many years ago when I dealt with the death of my parents. "Revenge doesn't help bring closure. You can still hold them responsible but know that you are not judge and jury. Actively seeking revenge will not help. It merely holds you back."

That counselor could kiss my ass. For Silas, I was going to be judge, jury, and executioner. Or I would join Brittany trying.

Before that, though, Jax, Niki, and Nate needed our help. Josh, Thomas, and I had no intention of leaving them to be exsanguinated to feed Silas's army. We knew where they were being held. Club Starlight. I had visited that club only a few days before. Before I realized what Silas was. Before I learned about the whole dark world that existed just under everyone's reality. A world where monsters existed, and legendary emperors made blood pacts with them.

My mind pulled up the layout of the club. If I had to guess, Silas held them in the upstairs management offices. Assuming he hadn't turned or corrupted all the staff, the offices provided the only sanctuary to hide them.

The more I pondered the rescue mission and our next moves, the more I felt myself slipping into this new reality. *I'm not a part of this world*, I kept telling myself. Vengeance drove me. Revenge motivated me to keep going. I needed the Night Crew to accomplish my goal. After I put Silas's head on a spike, I walk away.

The drone of the road continued.

On autopilot, I turned the car onto the unlit road. In what felt like an instant, my arms turned us into the warehouse parking lot.

The lights inside the warehouse lit up the entrance. As I pulled to a stop, Thomas leapt out of the passenger seat and stood at the entrance in a blinding flash of speed. I opened the door and stepped out.

"Everything ok?" I asked him.

"Yes," he said. "I saw movement from inside."

When I arrived at the entrance, Josh was in his wheelchair with a bag on his lap. He picked up a few items from the floor and placed them in the bag. "I thought I told you to get some rest," I hollered as Thomas and I strode to him.

"Intel called. Since this site is compromised, they identified an alternate secure site. Intel wants us to move tonight," Josh said. He spun around and headed back to the meeting area. "I have just about everything we need for now already. Oh, Mike. Intel left a note for you."

He grabbed the note off the conference table and handed it to me.

"Thomas, can you help out with anything Josh has left to grab."

I read the note, grabbed my cell phone, and dialed Austin.

"Mike, I have a plan," he said.

After a few adjustments, I hung up the phone and joined Thomas and Josh outside. The back of my car sat noticeably lower than before.

I pointed to the trunk. "Did you guys grab enough stuff?"

"I would have brought more if we had one of the SUV's," Josh said. "Are they both out of commission?"

"Last time I saw the one Scott and I drove, it was working. I'm not sure what may have happened to it since. We can grab it in the morning. We'll need it for the rescue."

"Do we have a plan?" Josh asked.

"Yeah, we have a plan."

32

The line into Club Starlight extended down the sidewalk. Men and women in their twenties stood waiting for their turn to enter, dressed up for a night of drinking and dancing. Almost everyone wore either long sleeves or a jacket thanks to the unseasonably cold weather.

I stood midway down the sidewalk with Thomas directly behind me. He still wore his black trench coat and boots, but he'd changed his shirt and jeans. He'd also slicked back his jet-black hair and tied it up in a ponytail. I wouldn't have been able to pick him out of a crowd.

Earlier that day, after everyone had rested in the new safe house, I went over the plan again with Thomas and Josh. Josh made the necessary arrangements while I went with Thomas to retrieve the SUV that was left by the farmhouse.

Everything looked so different in the daylight compared to the darkness of last night. Last night's claustrophobic tree line sat a few feet from the gravel road. Seeing it now, though, I realized it was an illusion. Only a few rows of trees opened to wide fields on both sides, not deep dark forests.

The SUV sat untouched along with the gear in the back. I looked around for signs of Scott but found nothing. Only the SUV, parked in solidarity, on the gravel road. I tossed Thomas the keys. He drove it back to the safe house, and I drove to HQ to pick up a few things for tonight.

For the evening, I bought a trench coat of my own to match Thomas. I purposefully bought it a size too big so it draped loose across my shoulders. Standing in the cold night air, the coat kept me warm and concealed what I needed it to.

"Why's it so busy tonight?" I asked the guy in front of me. He looked to be in his mid-twenties. He wore dark jeans and a Punisher T-shirt. A wide belt buckle kept the shirt up in the front. Ah, Texas. We love our belt buckles. "What's the occasion?"

"They posted all over social media. Tonight only. No cover and half priced drinks all night. Also, some people will get a special stamp for free drinks. My goal is to drink enough that I won't remember tonight," the guy said. He smiled while he talked, excited for the evening ahead.

"Maybe you'll get the special stamp," I said.

"I wish. I'm sure that's just going to the hot chicks."

Josh spoke up in my ear. "Silas wanted to pack the place."

"Discount enough," I commented quietly, "and no matter the night, he'll have the place packed."

"Everything's all set on my end," he said. A quiet rumble made its way through the earpiece. "How're you two looking?"

I glanced toward the entrance. Twenty people stood in line in front of us. I relayed that to Josh.

"Thomas, are you picking up anything?" Josh asked.

The club's music had a loud, rhythmic bass line which bled into the parking lot.

"There's going to be too much for my senses to be of much help. Once we get in, I'll be able to see before I can hear or smell."

"Remember the mission objective," I said. "Find and secure Niki, Nate, and Jax, and then put a stop to Silas's recruitment party. Stick to the plan as much as we can. Improvise only when necessary."

"We're assuming that Silas is here, right?" Josh asked.

"He's here," Thomas said. "I can feel him."

I felt the same way. Silas wouldn't want to miss out tonight. He'd want to be in the middle of it, running it, leading it, making sure everyone has him to thank for this revolution.

"We're next," I said quietly. "Game time."

We both pulled out our ID's and stepped just inside the door. On our right, a petite brunette stood behind the counter. She wore tight cowgirl jeans and a crop top that highlighted her flat stomach. I handed her my driver's license. She took a quick look at it, then me, then handed it back to me. She turned my hand over and stamped the back of it.

Thomas followed suit behind me, and she did the same to him. Thomas tapped me on the shoulder, and I turned to him. He pointed to the left just inside the club to a bouncer standing by a staircase. According to the club plans we reviewed earlier today, that staircase led upstairs to the management offices. His appearance cautioned anyone who wanted to make a trip upstairs.

I glanced back at Thomas, and he held up two fingers in a peace symbol next to his chest. For us, though, that didn't mean peace. That meant V for vampire.

Game on.

I took a deep breath and strode over to the beast of a man standing there. Thomas disappeared into the swarm of bodies in the opposite direction.

"Godspeed," came his voice in my ear.

"Amen," Josh responded. His voice sat just louder than the rumble coming from his end.

The large vampire ignored me as I approached. He kept looking out over the crowd of people until I stood directly in front of him. I grabbed the front of his jacket with both hands, giving it a tug. His torso didn't budge, but he dropped his head and eyes to peer down at me. His nose curled up in anger wondering why someone would be stupid enough to touch him.

"Hey, big guy," I said. "Your boss is looking for me."

33

The bouncer's eyes doubled in size as he realized who I was. He raised his hands and placed them on top of mine. His hands swallowed mine. There was a great deal of pressure as he began to squeeze.

I quickly let go of his jacket.

The bouncer released my hands and grabbed the front of my trench coat. He started to lift me off the ground.

"Hey now. I'm going willingly. Why don't you just point me in the right direction instead of carrying me?"

He sat me down and gave a half smile revealing razor sharp teeth. He took a step to the side, pointing up the staircase. "Door at the top," he said in a deep voice. "Silas will be happy to see you."

At least he confirmed our assumption that Silas was here.

I forced my legs up the staircase. Talking through the plan and actually doing it felt like two very different things at that moment. The man who killed my wife waited just beyond the door at the top of these stairs. The man who held my new friends captive, waited there for me.

The music blared behind me, and the lights flashed. A red hue bounced off the walls.

Only paint.

Despite the music, I heard the steps creak and groan on each step my feet landed. Each wooden plank felt like a step closer to my end. I believed in the plan, but even best laid plans could fail.

Have faith, Brittany's voice echoed in my head.

Even in this moment, I felt her next to me.

With a last deep breath, I stood in front of the door. "Here goes nothing," I whispered.

"You're not alone," Josh said.

I needed that reminder. At this moment, it certainly felt like me versus a room full of vampires, one of which was an extremely powerful alpha who wanted to upset the status quo and lead a revolution.

I turned the doorknob and threw open the door.

Immediately, the smell of old cigar smoke engulfed my senses. The carpet didn't help. It must've endured decades of spilled alcohol. The smell hit me in the face like a well-delivered right hook. The only thing that helped was thinking about how Thomas would've reacted to it.

Straight across from the door, I saw the glass windows overlooking the dance floor. The colors pulsating with the music illuminated the office area. A few couches and chairs, a few poles, and a bar dotted the large room. For an office area, there seemed to be a lack of computers, filing cabinets, or even a desk. I guessed this served as more of an elite suite than an office.

The door slammed into the wall as I threw it open. "Lucy, I'm home!" I yelled, making sure I had the whole room's attention.

Peering around, I counted six people in the room. Silas stood next to the glass, gazing out over the dance floor. Three others—I assumed vampires—spread out between two couches. Another sat on an overstuffed chair. A different chair held the familiar face of John Jennings.

In the corner by the bar, Jax, Nate, and Niki stood with their arms above their heads, suspended from the ceiling. Tubes ran from their sides into bags at their feet. IV bags attached to their arms kept them hydrated. Their bloodied faces hung to the ground. They looked weak but alive.

"Mr. White," Silas said and turned away from the glass wall to look at me. "Michael. Nice of you to join us."

The four vampires in the room stood up quickly. Jennings didn't move.

"Gentleman," Silas continued, "don't just stand there. Get our honored guest a chair."

One of the four grabbed a folding chair against the wall and sat it down between them. Silas flopped down on the couch.

I moved over to where Jennings sat. "You're in my chair. He brought yours," I told him.

Jennings glanced over at Silas who cocked his head, telling him to move. Jennings stood up in front of me, his rotund stomach brushing against me, and went to the folding chair. I sank into the cushioned chair.

"Thanks, Detective. Hey, how's your hand doing?"

"I heard about your interrogation methods," Silas interrupted. "I have to say, I like your work."

I could tell by Jennings's face he didn't appreciate Silas giving me kudos for putting a knife through his hand. The memory caused him to rub his injured hand with the good one.

"Well, I also told him if I saw him again, I'd kill him. I like to keep my promises, so let's see how the night goes."

"Indeed," Silas said. He smiled, enjoying himself as we sat across from each other. "I thought you might be here tonight, but I must admit, I didn't think you would just walk in. I'm assuming you want to make a trade. Your life for theirs?"

"Benji," I started.

The smile on his face immediately disappeared as I butchered his birth name.

"I see you've chatted with my brother," Silas interrupted. "Is he here with you somewhere? I doubt you would come here alone." He motioned to two of the vampires and pointed at the door. They stood and marched out of the office, heading downstairs.

"Now, if you want to negotiate, I suggest you show a little more respect."

"Respect? So jumping Scott and me in the dark is respectful? Ambushing the others is respectful?" I felt my anger growing. "Weren't you raised during a time when armies met on a battlefield, stood in front of each other, and started shooting?"

"Continental warfare was foolish. Civilized war, they called it. Nothing civil about it. Respect is understanding the power of the person you are speaking with." Silas stood from the couch, slithering closer to me as he spoke. "Respect is not having a lesser species dictate what you can or can't do. Do humans ask the cows or chickens how many of their kind they can kill? Do humans wait for the fish to tell them if they can reproduce? No. Yet, we have weak leaders who listen to our food supply. Oh, and if we disobey our cattle, those same leaders provide our cattle with the means to hunt us."

Silas stood directly in front of me. He placed his hands on the arms of the chair and leaned directly into my face. His red eyes burned into me.

I bottled my anger. "What makes you the savior of the vampires? I've heard there were others before you. They failed."

"Yes, in the past, but look around you today. No one even believes in us anymore. I'm a shadow. Vampires are make believe, only found in books and movies. We sparkle or are sex symbols."

He stood back up and paced the floor. "Even the Council is weak. The Accords are finally crumbling. I'm going to show other like-minded rebels it can be done. We are the dominant species."

"Just you vampires or everything that goes bump in the night?" I asked. I continued to sit relaxed and composed in the cushioned chair.

"It's freedom for all, but vampires *are* the dominant species," he said.

"So you are going to ask the werewolves to trade one master for another, making yourself that master. And it's all starting with whatever you are doing here tonight?"

"The recruitment party," he said, smiling again. He strolled to the glass wall, placed his hands on the pane, and gazed out over the crowd of people underneath. "It's almost time."

"Mike," Thomas said in a whisper in my ear. "I've counted less than a dozen vampires in the room, not counting the two I've already disposed of. I'm in position."

I spun the chair around to face Silas and the glass wall. I pointed at my friends in the corner. "Have you taken enough from them? If you want me, they stay alive."

"They're fine," Silas said. "I've done this long enough to know what's too much. Jax is as hard to kill as I am."

"Why do you want me?"

"I've wanted you for many years," he said. "You have a gift. One that'll come in handy when my reign begins. I felt it when you first stumbled into my sanctuary."

"Into your sanctuary?" I said almost in a daze.

The darkness from the one black spot in my memory became less dark. The red eyes in the tunnel. Was it a tunnel? It seemed bigger now. A hallway almost. Martin screamed for help. Silas! Did he find us, then?

"It's time," he said, still staring out over the multitude of people below him. He pointed to the other two vampires in the room. "You two stay here with him. You, as well, Detective. You can watch the show from up here."

Silas backed away from the glass and proudly stuck his chest out. He got to the door, opened it, and strode downstairs, closing the door behind him as he did.

34

I moved over to the glass wall as he maneuvered his way through the sea of dancers toward the front of the stage. The large bouncer helped to part the waters as he made his way to the DJ booth. Silas jumped up on the stage and reached his hand toward the DJ. The DJ turned the music down and handed Silas a microphone.

As soon as the music died down, everyone stopped moving and turned their attention to the front. Hundreds of people stood gazing up at the gaunt figure with long brown hair, holding the microphone.

I scanned the crowd searching for Thomas but couldn't find him.

"Welcome to Club Starlight!" Silas shouted into the microphone. "Are you having fun?"

A powerful cheer shook the walls of the club giving Silas a wide grin.

With the music off, the screen behind him showed an assortment of colors slowly pulsating to no particular rhythm as if it was lost without its accompaniment. Spotlights from high above still danced over the crowd in front of Silas.

"I'm glad to hear," he continued. "I have only a few more announcements before we get back to the festivities. First, if you've loved the drink specials so far, just wait. When I leave the stage, all drinks are...", he paused, "...on the house."

Another loud cheer erupted.

I realized there was a secret message in what he said. That announcement belonged to the dozen hidden patrons within Club Starlight who Thomas had identified, not to the few hundred standing at Silas's feet. A recruitment party? Silas intended this to be more like a forced conscription.

Another cheer erupted, bringing me out of my thoughts. Stick to the plan.

"And lastly, I have a special surprise for you," Silas said.

"Now, Thomas," I quietly said.

This afternoon, as the three of us huddled over a small folding table in the living room of the safe house, we had went over the plan for what felt like the thirtieth time. Thomas had asked why he had to do this part of the plan.

"I'm not like him," he had said. "I prefer to not be the center of attention."

"Thomas," I urged. "I need the distraction. If Silas is there, which I'm a thousand percent certain he will be, *he's* going to want to be the center of attention. Intel, and I as well, anticipate they are being held here." I pointed to the management office on the blueprints of Club Starlight that lay sprawled across the small table. "I won't be alone, though. You are creating my window of opportunity."

"I see that, but it doesn't mean I have to like it."

"Brother!" Thomas yelled.

The shout reverberated in my ear leaving a ringing. It also echoed on the bottom floor of Club Starlight.

The party goers turned in confusion, unable to find where the pronouncement came from. I also searched for Thomas in the dancing spotlights of the crowd but couldn't see him. After a few moments of confusion, a couple of people in the center of the crowd pointed upward. At first, I thought they pointed at the glass of the management office and at me, until I more closely followed the growing number of stares and points.

Thomas Price stood on top of the light array that hung immediately over the bar, illuminating it. The bar, which sat in the middle of the club just before the expanse of the dance floor, put Thomas directly in line with Silas.

The brothers stood opposite each other with a sea of innocent people between them.

"Brother!" Thomas yelled again. "You really love hearing yourself talk, don't you?"

The two vampires in the room with me hurried to the glass wall. Jennings joined them, watching the two brothers. I slowly backed away, hearing everything in my earpiece and through the office speakers.

"Thomas," Silas said. "I heard you may be here. Ladies and gentlemen, this is a rare occasion. My brother doesn't like to be out amongst people much. Can I get a round of applause for him?"

The crowd gave a tepid reply.

Silas, obviously wanting to show his control over the masses, said, "Oh, you can do better than that. Ladies and gentlemen, my brother, Thomas!"

The crowd erupted in cheer.

Jax raised his head up at the sound of Thomas's name. He stared directly at me, and I saw lucidity in his eyes. Although he had lost a lot of blood, I knew he could still fight.

I motioned my head toward Nate and Niki suspended on his left side and put a finger up to my mouth so he knew to be silent. Jax nodded in understanding while I kept inching my way toward them.

He slowly moved his leg out and kicked Nate. Nate gave a soft moan, but the three by the window paid more attention to what was happening below them. Jax kicked a little harder, and Nate raised his head toward him. Jax motioned his head in my direction causing Nate to look at me.

I opened my trench coat that hung too big on me, showing the two of them what I had hidden inside.

"Oh, brother," Thomas yelled from on top of the bar. "If only these unsuspecting people knew what you had in store. Do you really think they want what you have to offer?"

"I'm counting on it. What do you all think? Are you ready for your final surprise?" Silas goaded the audience, teasing them with the prospect of even more than no cover charge and now free drinks.

Nate used his leg to get Niki's attention while I continued to inch closer. When she didn't initially respond, he kicked harder. Very softly, I barely heard her Australian accent. "I'm awake and that hurt, you ass."

"Without further ado," Silas began.

From above us, I heard running water. I gazed out over the swarm of people and saw the sprinkler system kick on. Each sprinkler head above the entirety of the club erupted. A flood of red liquid rained down.

"It's blood," Thomas said. "He's dousing everyone with blood."

"Josh, light 'em up," I said.

35

Some of the people on the dance floor moved out of the way, taking cover. Others reveled in the deluge, gyrating as the DJ cranked up the music. The music drowned out the initial screams.

From above, I watched as a handful of people on the dance floor fell to the ground. The solid group of dancers suddenly had ten holes. The first screams came from next to one of the holes. As the crowd moved away, vampires feasted on the partygoers. One of the vampires lifted his head as blood dripped from his elongated incisors before bearing his head into the victim's neck again, ripping it open. A panicked mob rushed toward the doors only to find them locked.

Silas stood on the stage, blood from the sprinklers flowing down his face. His red eyes blazed as he surveyed the carnage happening below him.

Vampires engorged themselves on members of the crowd. People clutched at their throats with blood pouring from between their fingers. When a person fell, unable to carry themselves any further, a vampire would bite into their own wrist and shove it into the person's mouth.

Forced recruitment. Silas powered up his troops with the sprinkler-filled blood, allowing them to rip through the crowd, feasting on whoever they wanted, then force-feeding them vampire blood. Without help, hundreds of innocent people would be killed or turned.

The entire dance floor washed in red. The lights above still circled, highlighting the slaughter. We all needed to move fast to minimize the massacre. Thomas was the only one in that part of the club. It was up to him to slow down the vampires long enough so that the bystanders could escape. My heart pounded in my chest.

Thomas hopped off the light fixture above the bar and pulled out his machete. He ran at Silas, but a vampire covered in fresh blood left the body of a blonde woman on the floor and intercepted him.

I heard tiny explosions in the air conditioning vents against the back wall. In my earpiece, I heard the rumble that accompanied Josh become the full roar of an engine. Josh kicked in his part of the plan.

I ran to Jax. As I did, I opened the front of my coat, tossed it down, and pulled out two silver grenades. Just as the two vampires turned away from the window, I lobbed the grenades over my shoulders, and the room exploded with a dense fog of silver nitrate. The combination of my grenades and what came through the vents coated the air so thick that my own esophagus felt rough with each swallow. The vampires immediately began coughing and clawing at their throats. They carved large gash marks into their necks, searching for relief from the burning chemical.

From my back, I grabbed the machete strapped there *Die Hard* style, ripped it off of my shirt, and cut through the cords holding Jax's arms above his head. After spinning around with the blade, Nate and Niki's arms also fell to their sides.

All three briefly dropped to the ground. When they stood up, they removed the IV bags and the surgical tubing. Blood started to ooze from their fresh wounds.

"Can you walk?" I asked.

"We'll make do," Jax said.

"What's next?" Niki asked.

I reached behind my back into my belt and pulled out her silver whip. She grasped it with a smile. "Next we take care of the few up here. Thomas is trying to help downstairs. Josh is making a door."

"Making a door?" Nate asked as he stood.

From the glass window, we saw silver mist pump in through the air conditioning vents above the dance floor.

Earlier that day, with the blueprints laid out, Josh had circled the best locations to place the silver grenades. "A place that big has to have a robust air conditioning system. As long as you have them in these places, I can remote detonate them. In minutes, there'll be enough smoke that it'll be hard for non-vamps to breathe. Speaking of," Josh had said. He reached down next to his chair and tossed a respirator to Thomas. "You'll want to put this on. It's going to get rough for you in there, but this'll keep you from dying."

Like Josh had said, within moments, a dense fog lay across the dance floor and upstairs office. It made the large display screen against the back wall behind the DJ barely visible. The spotlights continued to dance beams of light randomly across the floor.

I helped Jax, Nate, and Niki onto their feet. As I did, I heard footsteps coming quickly our direction. Just as the first vampire became visible in the fog, I grabbed the machete and swung hard as if swinging a baseball bat and hitting a home run. The body ran three more paces before dropping to the ground. His head fell to the carpet at my feet.

Niki straightened out her whip as the second one appeared. She caught him first by the arm with it, spinning him around closer to us. Nate kicked as hard as he could into the vamp's chest, sending him back another five feet. With her second attempt, her whip landed around his neck. She flicked her wrist, and the head and body separated, rolling in two different directions.

"What the hell!" Jax said, moving to the glass wall.

From across the club, the barely visible display screen started to ripple. Silas turned to look up just as the first bricks fell. Before he could move out of the way, the wall buckled, burying him under a pile of cinder blocks. The bulldozer Josh drove broke through the wall, sending more blocks cascading down on top of the DJ booth and Silas.

Once the wall collapsed, the power inside the club went out. Emergency lighting kicked on, providing the only illumination for downstairs. Upstairs, the few flickering emergency lights had little impact in the silver fog.

The tide of people rushed across the club, climbing over rubble and escaping into the cold night air. They ran past Thomas as he worked his way through the crowd. He found a vampire writhing on the dance floor, unable to do anything except scratch at its throat. He gripped the vampire's hair and lifted it up. With one swipe from his machete, the head fell away from the body. A lady screamed as Thomas held the severed head. Blood dripped from the exposed neck, adding to the already blood-soaked dance floor.

I could only imagine the nightmares people were going to have. The blood drenched floor, headless bodies squirting blood, their friends' throats ripped open. Any one of those things would cause the sanest person to have a lifetime of therapy appointments.

At least people who needed therapy appointments meant they were still alive. I focused on that aspect of it. They survived.

I shifted my focus back to the fog-filled room and the task still needing to be done.

Niki and Nate hurried to the door of the office. They found it locked, so Nate kicked it open. Jax followed close behind as they started down the stairs. I paused.

Jax turned to look at me. "You coming?"

"Yeah, I'll be right there. One last thing to take care of."

36

Jax shrugged and took off behind Nate and Niki. I glanced past the glass, watching them join the throng of people leaving through Josh's new door. When they reached Josh, Nate helped him off the bulldozer, and the four of them formed a circle for a group hug.

"Thomas," I said into my earpiece. "If you are good, head out. Help them to the vehicles before Silas can dig his way out. I'll be there shortly."

With everyone to safety, I maneuvered to the door and closed it. An eerie silence settled upstairs. The gray fog and extremely low visibility caused sensory deprivation. I placed my back against the wall by the door. My right hand still clutched the machete.

"Detective?" I listened for a response; any sound or movement to signal where he was. "Are you still up here? The door was locked so I'm guessing so."

With my eyes closed, I used my perfect recollection to see the room. The couches sat directly in front of me. I could see the location of the overstuffed chair I sat in earlier.

I moved to my right toward the middle of the room, still keeping the door close behind me. "Marco?"

Click!

Quickly, I dropped to the ground as the gun fired. The bullet whizzed just over my head. He fired again in my direction. This time I saw the muzzle flash. He stood next to the glass wall by the bar.

"I told you I'd kill you if I saw you again," I hollered from the carpet. The stench of alcohol filled my nose. I almost gagged breathing it in.

"You're all alone, Mike," he shouted. "No vampire to back you up."

"I didn't need one in the car, and I won't need one, now."

He fired again. The bullet flew closer to me, but still too high.

I rolled to the couch and crawled as low as I could get. Memories of basic training crept into my head. Barbed wire strung above me, covered in mud, and my face continuously slipping into the water underneath me. I never thought I'd be using that same technique outside of the military.

Still crouched low, I passed the last couch, bringing myself closer to the bar. The silhouette of John Jennings came into view. He trained his gun at the door still, waiting for me to make a sound. Like a lion, I slowly inched; one hand closer on the carpet followed by a foot.

Only a few feet separated us. If he turned in my direction, he would see me almost on top of him. As I positioned my left leg underneath me, my knee gave an audible crack.

Fuck, I'm not that old yet.

Then he spun around.

In an instant, I leapt toward him with the machete clutched in both hands. I meant to drive it down through his skull. He quickly turned the gun in my direction and fired. The bullet tore through the right sleeve of my shirt and scraped just over my shoulder. I lost the grip on the machete and sent it hurling into a glass pane behind him.

My combat training kicked in, and muscle memory took over. My left hand shot out, grabbing his wrist, while my right fist collided with his chest. His chest and shoulders collapsed in as the oxygen suddenly evacuated from his lungs. My body spun, and my right hand replaced my left on the arm with the gun. As I turned, my right leg extended for a round house. I caught him in the stomach and sent him backward.

As Jennings stumbled backward, I saw spider webbing in the glass pane from the machete. Jennings tried to use the glass wall to stop himself. As he fell into it, the glass exploded around him. He disappeared out of the management office. Moments later, I heard a cracking thud.

Slowly, I went over to the shattered window and glanced over the edge. Jennings landed with his head facing the ceiling. His legs lay on top of a table with his back bent awkwardly off the edge.

He didn't move.

Touching my shoulder, I winced at the pain. Blood stained my shirt around the tear. My feet led the way to the door. I opened it and slowly trudged down the staircase to the first floor. The sprinklers shut off as I reached the bottom.

Almost everyone had filtered out of Club Starlight. Only a few dozen people left waiting their turn to climb the mound of cinder blocks and rubble and race to their car for safety.

I went to the detective's body; trails of blood flowed from his mouth and nose.

No eternal life for you. Hope it was worth it.

Pools of blood from the sprinklers dotted the dance floor. The sound of liquid spilling from tables and chairs engulfed the inside of the club. How many people had Silas drained of blood to create this mess? I tried not to think about that or the number of dead in here as I stalked past the bar.

Dozens of bodies lay strewn across the dance floor. The headless had been dispatched by Thomas. The others, though. Most had chunks of their throats ripped out. They lay scattered on the ground with terrified expressions plastered on their faces. Their mouths hung open in silent screams, and their lifeless eyes stared into nothing. There were so many victims we couldn't save. Although I knew we saved over a hundred, it didn't make seeing the dozens dead any better.

The last of the crowd escaped through the hole in the wall as I arrived at the front of the stage. I stopped, listening to the rubble.

"Silas," I said, standing there. "I know you aren't dead and can hear me. You'll find a way to get out of there soon, I'm confident. Hear me when I tell you, I'm coming for you when you do. You should've taken me that night instead of my wife."

I stepped onto the stage like the panicked crowd before me. As I did, I heard a block fall onto the dance floor a few feet away from me.

He's already digging out.

I grabbed the edge of the wall and hoisted myself around the bulldozer.

The chill night air struck my face. I took a deep breath of fresh air. No ancient cigar smoke or carpets soaked with alcohol. Beautiful October night air.

Cars spilled out of the parking lot, and in the distance, the sound of wailing sirens grew louder. Someone had called the authorities. I couldn't imagine what the news would say. Although if I had to guess, Intel probably had contingencies for that.

In the back of the parking lot, the SUV and my black Acura sat idling, waiting for me.

37

I cracked open a window letting some of the brisk morning air fill the small safe house. Standing in the living room with my coffee mug clasped between my hands, I paced from the living room, into the small kitchenette, and back to the living room.

Austin, or Intel as the Night Crew knew him, had found this small house after Silas and company destroyed the warehouse. It worked as a temporary location, but that was about it. The house had three bedrooms, making sleeping quarters for the six of us cramped.

On one of my pacing rotations, when I stepped between the living room and kitchenette, I glanced down the hallway at the bedrooms. The hallway stayed dark, and the doors were all shut. Thomas had taken the night watch while I had fallen asleep on the couch. Nate and Niki had the master bedroom, Jax slept in the second bedroom, and Josh in the third.

In the living room, the television played the local news, and I listened for reports about last night. I started toward the kitchenette when the first report came on.

"An update on the late-night fire at Club Starlight," the young, brunette news reporter said. The first rays of sun illuminated the sky behind her. She stood in front of burnt remains that I could only assume used to be the club. An occasional whiff of smoke escaped from the rubble.

"Fire investigators have just begun their inquiry into whether this was an accident...or arson. According to eyewitnesses, although the sprinkler system did come on, a red substance sprayed out which experts say could point to extremely rusty pipes helping to contribute to the blaze. So far, the death toll of this tragic event stands at forty. Megan, back to you."

The picture flipped back to an older lady in a blue, form fitting dress sitting behind a desk. "Thanks, Kelly." A picture of a young Detective Jennings in his police uniform popped up in the upper corner of the screen. "John Jennings, a local detective, was among one of the fallen last night. Our hearts and prayers go out to his family as well as all of the families impacted by this tragedy." She briefly paused. "Now over to Robert for today's weather. Rob, will this cold front stick around much longer?"

I paced back over to the kitchenette, still sipping on my coffee, and let the weather report fade into background noise. A map of the city lay sprawled across the table with a knife stabbed through each corner securing it. I sat in a chair and leaned over the map. A black sharpie sat in the middle of it. I grabbed the sharpie and started circling different spots.

"What are you doing?"

I jumped out of my chair, spilling the last of my coffee on my shirt. I spun around and saw Jax leaning against the hallway wall.

"You scared the shit out of me."

He pointed to my stained shirt. "Maybe switch to decaf. You are too wound up. Plus, vampires don't attack in the morning."

"Good to know. And decaf coffee kind of defeats the purpose of coffee, doesn't it?"

Jax smiled and gave a slight chuckle. "True."

He strolled over to the table and stared at the map and my circles. "And these are?"

I pointed at the different circles. "This is Club Starlight. Over here is the house where I went on the first raid with you. This is the farmhouse, and this is my house."

"All areas where you knew Silas has been at some point."

"Exactly. I was hoping to see if there was a correlation. Maybe he's staying somewhere in the middle. Unfortunately, these are all random, so that's a bust."

Jax went over to the kitchen counter, grabbed a coffee mug, and poured himself a cup of coffee. I sat back down at the table.

"Creamer in the fridge," I said.

"No thanks. Black works. Need me to top you off?"

"I'm good. That's the third pot I've made. No one helped me with the first two."

Jax shook his head. "How many times have you had to shit this morning?"

"Not enough." I leaned back in the chair.

He made his way to the table and sat across from me. "I never doubted you'd rescue us," he said nonchalantly while taking a drink of lukewarm coffee.

"Not at all?" I asked. I doubted I could rescue them, so it shocked me that he never did.

"Not in your DNA to have walked away. It's not part of who you are. I saw it in you immediately. That's why I had Nate and Niki tailing you. I knew you wouldn't walk away from your wife's murder, and I knew you wouldn't walk away from us. You're made for this, Mike."

"I..." I paused a moment. The words stuck in my throat. Finally, I said, "Thank you for that, but you're wrong. At least about the last part. You're right when you said I can't walk away. Not until I kill Silas for what he did to Brit. I'm done after that, though. Then, I am walking away."

"You're a great leader. If you decide differently, it won't be long before you have your own crew. For now, though, let's focus on stopping Silas." Jax leaned over the table, staring at the map. "Everyone else still asleep?"

"Niki and Nate are. Josh needed to grab a few things from the warehouse and took Thomas with him." Outside, I heard a door slam. "Speak of the devils."

A few moments later, the front door opened, and Josh wheeled himself in with Thomas, still in his dark coat, behind him.

"Get what you needed?" Jax asked.

"Of course, boss," Josh said. He reached down into his lap and held up vials of garlic extract and the syringe gun. "Shot for everyone to stay under the radar."

I leaned back in the chair again, grasped the seat underneath me, and gazed up at the cigarette smoke stained ceiling. Closing my eyes, I pictured the map of the city. Like zooming in on Google Maps, my image went from a bird's eye view to a street view. Growing up here, I knew the city as well as anyone. The street level map image sped through my head until I arrived at my house. From my house, I sped to the hotel where I had a room.

"Mike, are you ok?" Josh asked. "You have a death grip on your chair."

"Leave him be," Thomas said.

Like the Flash zipping through Star City, I flew past places I'd seen since I was a kid. Stores, restaurants, open fields that now contain parking lots for strip malls, and schools I attended. I saw them all.

I felt it so many years ago when you first stumbled into my sanctuary. Silas's words hung at the front of my mind.

I rewound the wheel of time and went back to my youth. The dark spot had to be what he talked about, but I couldn't access it. Did I see him before then? Where did Martin and I go?

Buildings deconstructed. 2022 disappeared and 1995 replaced it. I vividly remembered how the city looked and smelled when I was ten years old. The house I grew up in sat on the opposite side of town. My parents owned the house. My school sat two blocks over, and I rode my bike there every day, rain or shine.

Sweat dripped down my forehead, but I didn't care. I wasn't in the present anymore. My head found its way to another cold October on a Saturday morning. My mother made me put a jacket on that she had to get out of storage. It's Texas in October. Why would we need jackets already?

I stepped into the garage, shuffled over to the garage door, and unlocked it. My dad never installed a garage door opener. He said that's what I was for. I threw open the garage, and my best friend Martin stood in my driveway with his bicycle next to him.

"Come on, already!" he said. "I'm missing Power Rangers to show you this, you know."

"I'm missing it, too, butt munch," I said. "Where're you taking me?"

"It's a secret, but you'll love it."

I hopped on my bike, and we took off down the street. The memory grayed out, suddenly replaced by the sound of Martin's screams and the burning red eyes.

"Fuck!" I exclaimed and slammed the chair back down on the ground. I placed my arms on the table and rested my head in my hands. "I thought I had it."

"Are you ok?" Josh asked.

"Last night, Silas told me I stumbled into his sanctuary many years ago. His word. Sanctuary. I think that's when I first met him. In his hiding spot. I don't know if it's where he is today, but it's worth a shot. I just can't fucking remember it."

"Take a break," Jax said. "We'll find him."

"The memory is right there. It's like it wants to come out but it's blocked." A thought occurred to me. "Thomas, can you do that mind thing again and unlock it?"

"Mind thing?" Jax and Josh said in unison.

"After the headquarters was trashed, Thomas did some mind thing, and I saw through his eyes what happened that night."

I peered over at Thomas, and he held his head down, staring at the floor. Everyone else glanced between Thomas and me.

"What's the matter?" I asked.

Jax spoke up. "You couldn't even stand watching him drink from a glass, but you let him feed off of you?"

"Wait. What?" I asked startled.

"That's the only way it works," Josh said. "Once a vampire feeds off of you, there exists the connection to be able to do the 'mind thing'."

"Oh, I didn't know that," I said. "And he was dying!" I shouted out.

"No judgment from us," Jax said. "I'm glad you were there for him. I don't think any of us would still be alive if not for Thomas."

"I can try," Thomas finally said. "It's one thing to show you what I saw, to have you see through my eyes, but another thing to remove a shade from yours. Hopefully, since the memory wants to come out, there won't be any negative repercussions."

"Negative repercussions?" I asked hesitantly.

"Everything from pissing and shitting yourself to your body overheats and melts your brain out of your eyes," he said.

I looked at Jax, Josh, and Thomas in sequence. No one's expression changed. "Fuck me. I keep hoping when one of you says something like that it's a joke." I took a deep breath.

"I can handle it if I piss myself. Let's avoid having my brain melt out of my eyes. I like it where it is."

Thomas motioned to the couch, and I walked over. "You'll want to lie down."

My head felt the hard arm of the couch, and I shifted to get comfortable.

Thomas came over to me and kneeled on the floor next to the couch. He reached his hand out, but I grabbed it before he touched me. "Don't stop. Do you understand me? I need this memory. I can take it. Don't stop until the shade is gone."

Thomas gave a nod. He motioned for Jax to come closer. "Hold his legs," he said and placed his hand on my temple.

My body gave a huge jolt upward like I had been hit with electricity. I felt Jax grab my feet tighter, pulling my body back down to the couch. Intense pain radiated through my skull and then—

38

I pedaled fast on my BMX bicycle trying to keep up with Martin. At twelve, he was two years older than me and six inches taller. The Coopers lived three houses down from me. Separated by two grades meant we never saw each other during school.

The cool air burned in my chest on that Saturday morning in 1995. We went straight down the street, passing cars parked on the side or in driveways. The multicolored tree leaves littered the sidewalk. In the distance, I heard a few lawn mowers firing up to tackle their respective yards.

Martin slowed down as we approached an intersection. He waited a few seconds for me to catch up, then he turned left, heading into the next neighborhood. Street after street flew by. We went beyond the area we usually rode through, yet the houses all still looked the same. Street names changed, but the houses didn't.

I lost count of the number of intersections we crossed over before we turned left again, followed by a quick bank to the right. I popped my front tire up over the curb and landed it on the tall grass in front of an empty lot. Martin sat waiting for me on the other side of the lot in a field behind the row of houses. I pumped my legs and caught up to him.

The sweat of the ride plastered his red hair to his head.

"Where to next?" I asked, winded.

"Just a sec, I'm trying to remember," he said. He raised his hands to his forehead making a visor and peered beyond the field to a row of trees.

"We heading into the woods?" The nervousness in my young voice must have been audible.

"What's wrong, Mikey? Not scared, are you? I thought you were ten, not five like my little sister," he taunted.

"I am ten, and no, I'm not scared. And don't call me Mikey."

"Good," he said. "And I found the path. Come on. Don't slow me down, Mikey."

With that, he hopped back onto his bike and took off across the field. I stayed a few yards behind him, pedaling through the tall grass and weeds. The burrs scratched my ankles and stuck to my socks and shoes. Finally, we reached the entrance to the path leading into the woods.

"Where're we going?" I yelled at him.

Rocks made the trail incredibly bumpy. My tire bounced from side to side. A few times I felt the bike jar awkwardly and thought I'd wipe out. Fortunately, I didn't and stayed just behind Martin.

Suddenly, he skidded to a stop beside a chain link fence overgrown with weeds and vines. Twenty yards beyond the fence sat a dilapidated old building. Moss climbed the gray-toned walls. Broken windows with bars dotted the outside. The building looked about two stories tall. A loading dock split the building in half.

"What is this place, a prison?" I asked.

"My brother told me about it," he said. Martin's brother had a big mouth on him. He was five years older than Martin and loved to brag about everything from how much money he makes working at *Lowe's* to the number of girls he's dated.

"Bryan said it's where those kids died."

"Bullshit," I said. "That story isn't even real. Even if it was, they were found in the woods, not in some old building."

"Well, he said it was a big cover up, and now the building is haunted."

I stared at the broken-out windows of the building. A bird flew out of one and into the sky beyond.

"Haunted," I hesitantly said. "How do we even get in there?"

"The fence is torn over there," he said pointing a few yards away. "We'll have to leave our bikes here and walk over to it, though."

A lump formed in my throat. Leave our bikes here, crawl through a hole in a fence, and go into a haunted building where kids may or may not have died? Sure, that sounded like a great idea.

But, if I backed out now, I'd look like a baby. I could hear Martin ribbing me about it for the next few years. I swallowed hard to clear the lump out of my throat and took a deep breath.

We walked our bikes over to the hole in the fence and laid them down in the grass behind a tree. Martin reached for the fence and pulled back the loose part so I could fit through. It had obviously been cut away from the pole to make the opening.

"Ladies first," he said just as I slid through the opening.

"Asshole," I responded back.

Once Martin squeezed through the fence, we both stood and stared at the building. He hesitated before confidently striding through the high grass. I took a few quick steps to keep up with him.

"Did your brother tell you how to get in?"

"That door over there." He pointed to the one just beyond the loading ramp. "It looks shut, but the lock is busted."

The grass brushed against our legs, waving in the wind, as we approached the building. At one point, I heard a noise and froze.

Keep walking, you big baby. Not nighttime. Nothing to be scared of on a Saturday morning. No one gets killed while cartoons are playing.

A few steps later, the grass ended, and our feet hit pavement. After a quick run up the ramp, we stood at the door. Martin pushed it open with his shoulder, and the door swung inward with a loud groan. Rust particles fell off the inside, and I resisted the urge to cough.

"Want to go first?" he asked me.

I vehemently shook my head, despite the possibility of ribbing later.

"Baby," he said and stepped inside.

"Why do I even hang out with you?"

"Because I show you cool stuff like abandoned buildings where kids got killed," Martin said. He wasn't wrong.

I crept in after him.

The inside looked like a huge kitchen. Dull stainless-steel equipment sat all over the place. A counter with a sink and faucet sat on our right. On our left, cabinets and counters hung on the wall. Abandoned pots and pans dangled from a rack attached to the ceiling, slowly swaying in the breeze from the door like condemned men swinging by their necks.

The sunlight streamed in from the open door and illuminated a small path. Martin went first, and I stayed on his heels. With every step, we kicked dust bunnies into the air, making it sparkle around us.

Martin pushed the door to the exit, and it swung open easily. He stepped into a cafeteria with a stage across from us. I realized we were in an old school. The bars on the window made it feel like a prison, though. Suddenly, a loud bang rang out from behind us, and the stream of sunlight disappeared. We both jumped and spun around. The outside door had slammed shut.

"The wind," he said.

"Yeah," I agreed suspiciously. "The wind."

In my head, I prayed the wind shut the door and not the ghosts of murdered children locking us inside.

That's a myth, I kept telling myself.

Light shone into the cafeteria from the busted windows. The bars left shadows on the floor like prison cells. Long tables and chairs lay strewn haphazardly throughout the large room. The room stank of mold, mildew, and air that had sat still for ages. The smell permeated so heavily, I could taste the stench.

I don't want to be here, anymore. This place felt bad, felt wrong.

("Jax, keep holding him down. He's fighting the memory.")

"Martin, we should leave," I said. I tried to still the quiver in my voice with little success.

"Not yet. Bryan said the murders happened in the back hallway. That's where I want to go."

"Dumbass," I half whispered and half shouted to him. "Look around. See any footprints anywhere besides ours? Your brother hasn't been here. No one's been here for years."

"I don't care. I'm going, anyway," he said back and ran past the tables and chairs to the door at the far end of the cafeteria. He turned for a brief moment to look at me, then opened the door and disappeared into what lay on the other side of it.

He'd left me alone. My feet were glued to the floor, and my legs felt weighted down. Terror gripped me and didn't let go.

("Is he mumbling 'all alone'?" Jax asked. "Thomas, where is he?")

With every step, I forced my legs to do their job. I struggled with each step to the door Martin had run through. As scared as I was, I needed to find him. If I turned tail and ran back for the bikes, I'd never hear the end of it.

Slowly, I made my way to the door. Through a small window, I saw a dark hallway. I placed my hand on the doorknob, turned it, and stepped out of the cafeteria.

The door closed slowly behind me as I stood in the hallway, glancing up and down both ways. My head swiveled back and forth waiting for my eyes to adjust to the low lighting. The hallway extended both directions. To my right, it went to the end of the cafeteria before taking a sharp left turn. On my left, I saw a set of metal doors with small vertical windows in the center. A door leading into a set of offices sat on the left of the double doors. On the right side of the double doors, I saw more doors and another hallway.

I'm in an old school. It's just an old school.

("I think he's saying school now," Jax said.)

As my eyes adjusted, I peered down at the linoleum floor for Martin's footprints. Faintly in the dimness of the hallway, I found them heading to the right. I turned my body that way when I heard a scream.

My blood curdled as it echoed throughout the entire school.

Was that Martin?

I hoped it wasn't Martin, but if it wasn't him, I didn't want to meet what caused it.

Instead of freezing in place, I took off and sprinted around the corner. Lockers, one stacked on top of the other, lined both walls of the hallway, broken every dozen or so by a classroom door. Midway down the hall, I saw Martin in the grasp of a monster.

Martin's limp frame hung backward while the creature clasped onto his neck. Its long hair covered its face and dropped across Martin's back. The hands clutched Martin close to its body as it fed on him.

I had to save my friend.

"Let him go!" I yelled.

("Let him go?" Josh asked.)

("Hold him down," Thomas screamed.)

The monster glared at me. Its red eyes burned into me. It raised its head from Martin's neck and brandished its fangs still dripping with Martin's blood. It dropped Martin's limp body onto the dusty linoleum and stood upright. Martin's head bounced off the tile, and I saw him reach a hand to his bleeding neck. He was still alive. The bloodsucker made an audible sniff of the air and started walking to me.

"Martin, run!" I shouted and turned.

I sprinted around the corner, my feet almost slipping on the dirt and dust build up on the ground. I ran past the entrance to the cafeteria and headed to the doors at the front of the school. Behind me, I could feel the creature's breath on the back of my neck as if he hovered just above it. A stench I'd never smelled before emanated all around.

This must be the smell of death and decay like in those zombie movies.

The hallway opened on my right. I had no intention of going that way and kept to the front double doors. My hand stretched out to open the doors and freedom just beyond.

Moments before my hand hit the door, my direction violently changed. The monster grasped my shoulders and spun me around. I stared into the red eyes, watching as the fangs approached my throat. Sharp, piercing stings burned my neck. It reminded me of last summer when I was stung by a bee. I glanced down the hallway and saw Martin drunkenly stumble through the cafeteria door holding his neck.

As quickly as the bee stings happened, they stopped, and the creature pulled back, stumbled backward, and fell to its butt. "You have a gift," it said. "You have a power about you."

I took the opportunity to gather myself and bolt for the door. Two trails of blood trickled down my neck and stained the top of my shirt. Adrenaline drove me to keep running without hesitation.

My hands hit one of the double doors, slamming into the crash bar, and thrusting the door open with all my force. A chain stopped it from opening the whole way, but it moved enough to make a small gap. I forced myself through the gap, feeling the metal cut through my clothes and into my back. The pain was excruciating, but I pushed through. The warmth of the sun washed over me. I felt a sudden sense of safety and protection within its embrace.

Pushing through the door, I propelled forward. I lost my footing on the pavement outside and stumbled down the five steps in front of the school. The wind rushed out of me as my back collided with the cement ground. I stared at the building, squinting in the sunlight.

As my vision cleared, I read the large black letters suspended across the top of the building as a large shadow appeared above me. The beast stood between the school and me. But how? Sunlight should have saved me.

"I'm saving you for when you get older," it said. "I want your power to become strong." He leaned down and touched the side of my head. "But for now, I can't have you remembering where I live."

My eyes drifted back into my head as a grayness overtook the images in my mind. The grayness continued to darken until a gray tunnel turned to a black tunnel.

I opened my eyes to find the beast gone. In a daze almost like I was sleepwalking, I wandered through the overgrown grass. I found the hole in the fence that Martin and I slipped through not ten minutes ago. My bike leaned against the tree. Martin's bike was gone.

I grabbed my bicycle but didn't have the strength to throw my leg over it. I slowly walked back up the trail in my dream state. After what seemed like an eternity, the wooded trail opened into a field. I trudged forward with the bike still rolling along next to me.

Halfway through the field, I found Martin collapsed on the ground. His bike lay toppled on the ground next to him. The ground beneath his head turned a dark shade of red.

I looked up across the field to the street ahead. Houses surrounded the empty lot that we had ridden our bikes through. In the house to the right, I saw a man standing on a deck with a watering hose.

"Mister," I said. I thought I yelled it, but only a whisper came out. I fought the darkness of the dream; the tunnel in my vision narrowed further.

"Mister," I said only a little louder.

He continued to pay attention to the plants he watered.

The tunnel covered most of my sight. I only saw through a small dot.

Finally, I took a deep breath. The small light of the tunnel nearly closed up as the darkness swallowed me. "Mister!" I yelled and saw him raise his head as the tunnel collapsed, and I fell to the ground next to Martin.

39

I bolted upright and shot my eyes open, taking in a huge breath as if I'd been underwater.

Jax still held my feet down, and Thomas stood next to me.

"I remember!" I shouted.

40

As I stared at the rundown school in front of me, mixed feelings struck me. I felt whole but also a sense of dread. The memory of the frightened child had rooted itself in my head. It had dug deep and become a nagging spear.

Here, Silas had held me in his grasp and driven his elongated incisors into my neck. My life could've ended at the same time as Martin's did, yet Silas had stopped. What power did I possess that kept him from killing me?

Jax and Thomas waited next to me. Nate and Niki made their way down the side of the building to a door on the back hallway.

"I remember this place being so much bigger," I said. As a child, the front seemed to extend fifty feet into the air. "Why doesn't anyone else remember this place?"

Josh, from his place in front of multiple laptops at our temporary housing, chimed in. "If this is Silas's own personal hideout, I imagine the lengths he's gone to making it disappear are impressive. Even the city has no record of this place existing."

"How's that possible?" Nate whispered. I heard the leaves beneath their feet crunch as they walked.

"He bought a cop. How hard would it've been thirty or forty years ago to make a paper trail disappear? Especially before everything was digitized."

"Enough about the building," Jax said. "Sun is down, and the moon is out. Nate and Niki, I need you in position."

"We're almost there, boss," Niki said. "Do we even know if he's here?"

Thomas closed his eyes for a few moments. He took a deep breath and exhaled. "He's here. I can feel him." In the darkness, his eyes glowed light red.

I also took a deep breath, filling my lungs. I felt myself growing more and more anxious. "Tell me again why we're going after Silas at night when he's at full strength?"

"Because Thomas is also at full strength," Jax said. He took the first step forward, and Thomas and I followed suit.

Every pace drew us closer and closer to the doors. We climbed the few concrete steps, leveling us with the entrance. The sound of leaves crunching in my ear stopped. Nate and Niki stood at the side hallway door. The brisk air blew through the trees, and a full moon gave the only light. My heart beat in my chest so hard I thought it would explode out.

"Don't we want the element of surprise?" I asked.

Thomas grabbed the door handles, one in each hand. "Hell no," he said. "He knows we're here already." Thomas made a sudden movement, and a loud metallic explosion ripped through the air. The chain holding the doors together shattered. The doors flew off their hinges, and Thomas tossed them behind us. Metal rings from the chains fell to the ground.

A shotgun blast pierced my ears. "We're in," Nate said.

The shrieking sound of feedback reverberated from the intercom system. Jax, Thomas, and I glanced at each other in confusion.

"He must have an off-grid power supply," Josh commented as if he read our minds.

"Welcome to my humble abode," Silas said over the intercom. "It's been so long since the last time I had uninvited guests. Mike, how long has it been? Twenty years or so? Did the block finally wear off or did my dear brother unlock it for you? He tastes good, doesn't he, Thomas?"

"Come out here, you coward," Thomas yelled into the darkness of the hallways. His voice echoed down the empty corridors.

"Now, now. What fun would that be? I have so many fun surprises in store for you.

"Jax, you and your Night Crew have been getting better and better. The five of you against me doesn't sound fair at all. Maybe I'll trim the herd while you search for me. An old-fashioned hunt.

"Thomas, do you remember when we used to hunt prey together? The good old days before you hated yourself."

The intercom clicked off. A silence momentarily filled the hallways before Silas's voice blared through the intercom again. "Let the hunt begin." With that, the intercom clicked off a final time.

We stood silently in the entrance of the school. I turned on my flashlight and shined it down the hallway. The hallway extended straight, ending at two doors on the far end. The hallway turned into a T at the doors, splitting off into both directions. Next to where we stood, a wing of classrooms extended to our left. The front offices sat to our immediate right. A middle hallway also went left between the front and the back ones.

Silas could be anywhere.

Jax broke the silence. "Watch your backs. You heard him. For Silas, this is just a game, and we are in his house."

The three of us walked further into the building. Nate and Niki crept down the back hallway that made up the top part of the T. Jax pointed for me to follow him as we turned left down the front wing. He motioned for Thomas to go into the first room on the corner.

Thomas opened the door and stepped into the room. Despite the empty shelves, it looked like an old library. He eased the door closed behind him and disappeared into the darkness.

Jax and I walked the linoleum floor. He had his shotgun in his hand with the flashlight below it, illuminating our path. I had my pistol in one hand and a flashlight in the other. My muscles stayed tense as if ready to pounce at any moment.

Closed classroom doors lined both sides of the hallway. Jax went to the first door and motioned for me to take the one on the opposite side of the hallway. He opened his door and panned his flashlight across the room. I opened mine and did the same thing. The classroom gave off shadows at every turn. Empty desks sat covered in dust. I scanned the classroom, then crept back into the hallway, proceeding into the next room. We steadily made our way down the hallway.

When we only had four classrooms left, Nate spoke up in our ears. "First half of hallway is clear. The gym is just outside the double doors. I'm stepping out to check it."

"I've got the rest of the hallway," Niki said.

"Stay together, you two," Jax said.

I heard the back door open and quietly close. Nate must have eased it shut. "Entering the gym," he said.

"Nate, I'll head back to you," Niki said, acknowledging Jax's order.

The door creaked open. A large metallic crash sounded over the comm's. I jumped and Jax did the same.

"Sorry," Nate said. "The door slipped. I'm in a small entry way. The door to the gym is in front of me."

I heard a thud against a hard surface. I imagined Nate's shoulder hitting the door.

"It won't open," he said. "The door is solid metal. Heading back to you, Niki."

The crash handle of the exterior door depressed, but the sound of the door opening didn't follow it. The crash handle sound repeated multiple times. "Guys, I have a problem. The door won't open."

"Almost there," Niki said.

"Shit, hurry up. There's some kind of gas leaking in. I'm in a fucking mantrap here."

The outside door opened as Niki bolted to the gym. As Nate began to cough, Niki shouted, "Jax, someone help! The door won't open. He's trapped!" Niki pounded on the door with her machete, sending metal on metal screeching sounds over our comm's. "Hold on, baby! We'll get you out," she continued to shout. "Hurry! I can see him on the floor."

"Love you," Nate struggled to cough out.

"Thomas!" Jax shouted. "Thomas! I need you there, now!" Jax sprinted past me down the length of the hallway. When he reached the end, he turned left, heading to Niki and Nate.

No response came from Thomas.

I stood alone on the furthest side of the front hallway with the sound of Nate's coughing and Niki's sobs in my ear. Flashes of me as a child chased by Silas down these corridors popped into my head. Part of me wished I would've left that blank spot in my past alone.

Thomas should've been in the library. I headed that direction, quickly picking up the pace with each step. The library sat just to my left with the door facing the school's entrance. I pulled open the door and stepped into the darkness.

"Thomas," I whispered. "Where are you?"

My light danced back and forth across the room. The light shimmered off dust in the air. Empty bookshelves littered the library. The image of them made me think of skeletons. Hollow bones devoid of meat. The emptiness of the shelves allowed me to see across the entire library.

Where could Thomas be?

I walked backward to the door, still scanning the room. I glanced to my right and saw Thomas's earpiece sitting on a bookshelf that sat waist high.

41

I waited in the dark library to hear Jax make it to Niki, but he never did. Somewhere between here and the gym, something happened. Nate's coughing slowed to the point that I didn't hear it anymore. Niki's sobs were my only companion until they dissolved into the crackling of static.

"Josh, I'm getting interference," I said. After a few seconds of no response, I tried again. "Josh, can you hear me?"

Static filled my head. Empty, dead air.

As I stood alone in the library staring at Thomas's ear bud, the whole building felt dead. Darkness swallowed everything. Although the beam of my flashlight traveled through the empty shelves, it illuminated only a tiny fraction of the room as a whole. Anything could've been waiting for me just beyond its glow.

I reached behind me and felt for the library door. I pushed it back open and stepped into the hallway.

The static started to sputter. Pieces of words fought their way through. "—ott."

"Niki? I didn't catch that. What did you say?"

The static intensified again. Finally, I heard a word amongst the white noise.

"Scott."

"Niki, did you say Scott?"

Silence. Even the sound of static finally disappeared.

Standing in the hallway, I looked to my right past the classrooms Jax and I had just checked. Nothing. I was still alone. I turned to my left and crept down the long hallway toward the double doors. I passed the cafeteria entrance on my right. The middle wing of classrooms opened on my left. I stared down it, and my imagination took over. I saw Silas standing over Martin, draining him, killing him. The memory, foreign memory I didn't even know existed until today, hit me hard. I froze in the deep hole of the memory.

Keep going, Brittany's voice said.

I'm all alone against him.

You're never alone.

See anyone else in this hallway? I'm all alone except for the constant hallucinations of my dead wife's voice. Some hero I am.

Silas's voice suddenly echoed down the abandoned corridors. "Young Mr. White. By my count, you are the sole remaining member of the Night Crew. I expected so much more."

Don't listen to him, she said. *You are not alone.*

"Michael, we should just end this game now. I'm really very disappointed. I truly thought Jax trained everyone so much better than that. Accept your destiny, Michael."

Silas's voice helped pull me out of the memory hole. I blinked, and the vision of my childhood friend disappeared. My eyes briefly closed, and I took a deep breath of gratitude. I used the breath to center myself and clear my head. *Think, Mike. Think.*

Suddenly, a loud, metallic clang reverberated off the walls. I shot my eyes open, and jerked my head to the double doors. My mouth dropped open in shock. I couldn't believe my eyes.

Scott stood at the end of the hallway in front of the double doors. The last time I saw him, he was unconscious and being dragged away. He wore the same clothes as he did then except now his blue jeans had rips on the front and his plain white T-shirt had red stains spattered across it.

"Scott!"

He stood there and moved his neck in a circular motion, sending audible cracks through the silence of the building. "How's it going, Mike?" he asked. He smiled at me and revealed his razor sharp, elongated incisors.

Suddenly, Josh hollered into my ear. "Mike!"

I jerked my hand to my earpiece from the sudden shout.

"Is that Josh cowardly hiding somewhere far away?"

"That sounded like Scott. No one is responding. What's going on?"

"Josh, I'm the only one responding, right now," I said, staring straight ahead at Scott. He stayed against the back doors for now. "And yeah, that's Scott you hear, but Silas turned him."

"Just wait until you all join me. It's wonderful." He pointed at me. "He just wants you first."

"Mike, hang tight. I'm working on a plan."

"Work faster."

Scott spoke up before I could. "Working on some kind of plan, huh, Josh? I can almost hear you in Mike's ear. I hear everything so much clearer. I can hear your racing heart, Mike. I can see the blood pumping through your body, right now. Oh, and I definitely smell it." He took a big, exaggerated whiff of air through his nose.

I decided to do the only thing I could think of to bide Josh some time - taunt. "Scott, I'm guessing Silas sent you to bring me to him. Even as a vampire, you're an errand boy. What did Niki say when she first introduced us? You know a little about a lot but don't know shit about anything. Good to see nothing's changed."

"He just wants you alive to turn you. It shouldn't matter if I break your arms and legs in the process. Errand boy?" He steadily increased in volume and intensity. His eyes turned a deep red, almost crimson, as if they burned with the anger inside him.

While Scott yelled in front of me, I heard Josh whisper in my ear. He spoke quickly and quietly.

As Scott took a step forward, I turned to my left and sprinted down the middle hallway. I almost lost my footing on the dust-covered linoleum tile. Classrooms zoomed past me on both sides as I hoped to place some distance between us. Midway down the hall, I grabbed the doorknob to a classroom, using it to immediately stop my forward progress. I twisted the knob, opened the door, and quickly stepped inside, quietly shutting it behind me.

"Come out, come out, wherever you are," Scott sang down the hall.

I faced the door and concentrated on my breathing. I tried to slow it and my heartbeat down. I needed time, and if he heard me, Josh's plan wouldn't work.

I turned around and placed my back to the door. Immediately, my mouth clamped shut to suppress a scream at what I saw. The classroom contained six rows of desks with six to eight in a row. In each desk sat the skeleton of a child. Rags that were once clothes hung loosely from the dried bones. With no sinews to hold them shut, the jaws hung open as if locked in a silent scream. Cobwebs spanned between the remains and the desks themselves.

The stories from my childhood rushed back to me. Every generation had their tales of children who went missing and were never found. Those same stories had propelled Martin and I to seek out this building so many years before.

Silas had been hunting children for decades and storing their bodies here in this forgotten building. Who knows the countless numbers he drained prior to this building being built or where their bodies lay. How many other classrooms contained remains? None on the first hall had skeletons, but over thirty sat in front of me.

"Josh," I whispered. "If I make it out of here, remind me I need therapy."

A door opened a few classrooms down, then violently slammed shut. Scott was searching the rooms.

"Mike," Josh said. "I'll remind you to get whatever you need. Just make it out of there."

"Hey, Josh," Scott hollered. "I think after we turn the rest of Jax's Night Crew, we'll all come after you next."

He moved a classroom closer.

Josh spoke up in the earpiece, much louder this time. "Any word on Thomas? Do you have any idea where the others are?"

I didn't respond to Josh. Quietly, I crouched in the darkness.

"Keep talking, Josh. You are going to make it so much easier to find Mike."

"Intel has a drone in the air, and I have eyes over the building, now."

Scott's voice echoed down the hallway. "You aren't even making this hard." He threw open the door to the classroom I went into and shut it behind him.

Quickly, I moved into position and slid my machete out of its sheath.

"You sneaky son of a bitch," the vampire said.

Scott opened the door back into the hallway. As he stepped out, I swung the machete as hard as I could, sending it straight through his neck and burying it in the door frame. Scott's body fell to the ground. The head briefly rested on the blade before tumbling to the floor.

"Mike!" Josh said.

After dislodging the machete and placing it back in my belt, I stepped over Scott's decapitated body and walked to the middle desk in the first row. I reached down, grabbed the earpiece from on top of the desk, and placed it back in my ear. "I'm here. You can turn the volume back down. I can't believe that worked. I owe you one."

In the corner of the room, a doorway connected this classroom with the one next door. Josh had figured Scott would follow the sound, so he had suggested I leave the earpiece in one room, sneak back into the hallway via the connecting room, and catch Scott as he left. Josh had cranked the volume so Scott would hear him loud and clear.

"Best not to make a tally. Saving each other is part of what we do. In case you didn't hear, I have eyes in the sky now."

"Can you see into the building?"

"I just activated infrared. Mike, it's not good. You're in deep shit."

42

I took a deep breath. I didn't want to hear what Josh had to tell me. I already knew I was in deep shit. How could this get any worse?

"What do you see?" I finally brought myself to ask.

"I see someone in the gym, but there's no movement. That's probably Nate. Two warm bodies are in the cafeteria, and it looks like they're struggling against possible restraints. There's a blue there also."

"Is that Thomas?"

"The blue's marching around where the stage should be. My guess is that's not Thomas."

"Mine as well," I said. I felt defeated. After a pause, I asked Josh the one question I already knew the answer to. "One on one, I can't beat Silas, can I?"

"I..." he paused. The hesitation in his voice spoke more than any words he could have said. "We'll figure it out."

Standing in the classroom, surrounded by the skeletons of children who never had a chance against this monster, it felt as if the weight of the world rested on my shoulders. Silas wanted to start a revolution and topple the Council and the Accords. Anarchy. Monsters would run unchecked.

All revolutions started somewhere, and he picked here for his. He picked here to finally make his stand against Jax's Night Crew and

Thomas. He picked here to start his army, and he wanted me to be part of it.

With my back literally pressed against the wall, I slid to the floor. I sat there with my knees pulled up to my chest. Scott's headless corpse lay crumpled next to me. I buried my face in my hands and pressed my palms into my eyes. Death surrounded me.

I pulled my hands away and rested my head on the wall behind me. I could feel Silas waiting for me. I opened my eyes and fixated on the ceiling.

"Josh, you have the building plans, right?"

I heard clicking on the keyboard. "Yeah, what do you need?"

"From my current location, is there anything above me from here to the cafeteria?"

"Above you? Like in the ceiling?"

"Yes. Firewalls, cinder blocks, that kind of thing. If I go high, can I make it to the cafeteria?"

More clicking. After a few minutes, Josh answered. "The ceiling goes up about ten feet when you hit the cafeteria. It's raised for the lights and curtain above the stage. Other than that, nothing is in your way."

I stood and went to the desk closest to me. Looking at the small skeleton that sat in the chair and the tatters that was once a dress, I could imagine what the little girl looked like. I wished I could have saved her from the horror. Her eyes must have been filled with terror as Silas's red eyes burned in front of her before he drained her of her blood. Poor thing.

"Lord, have Mercy on her and all the children Silas preyed upon. I hope they found Peace with You."

"Amen," Josh responded.

I placed my foot on the seat of the desk, careful to not disturb the remains, and brought myself to the top of the desk. I pushed the ceiling tile up and out of the way. I felt for the rods holding the subceiling in place. Once I found one, I used it to hoist myself above the desks and into the dark abyss.

I climbed to the iron beams above the tiles and lay flat across them. With my flashlight, I surveyed my small crawl space. I needed to stay flat or risked bashing my head into more beams above me. If I slipped, I'd crash through the ceiling tiles.

"Josh, lead the way," I said.

"I see you on infrared. Turn to your right. The cafeteria is directly in front of you."

I twisted and let the beam of my flashlight illuminate the path forward. "I see where the ceiling goes up. Thirty feet sound about right?"

"That sounds about right."

Staying low, I crawled across the beams. My flashlight pointed straight ahead. I moved one hand forward, followed by a foot, then repeated with the other hand and foot. There was no reason to rush. If Silas wanted me so badly, he could be patient.

Traveling between beams while staying on my stomach, kicking up dust with every movement, the air grew thick, and I could hardly breathe. My arms trembled and sweat poured off my forehead. Was there a Camp Claustrophobia? If so, I earned that shirt as well.

Hey Brit, I could really use you, right now.

Silence. Of all the times I needed her company, this would've been a good one.

"Mike, you're making good progress," Josh said. "Unfortunately, I have more bad news."

"What could it possibly be? Swarm of locusts?" I stopped myself before I took my frustration out on Josh.

"Vamps. About a half dozen, maybe more. They are outside the school now but approaching."

"Okay. I can't deal with them, right now. I have to focus on Silas and saving the others." A thought occurred to me. "Josh, as much as I don't want to do this, I need to take the earpiece out."

"Mike, I think that's a bad idea."

"Scott could almost hear you. Silas will definitely be able to. If I even remotely want to get the drop on him, I need radio silence. Listen, Josh. Get Intel on the line. Tell Austin what happened. Hopefully another team can get here in time to stop Silas if things go bad. Stop objecting. I'm signing off. Thanks for everything, Josh."

His objections continued as I removed the earpiece and sat it on a tile. There were no more voices in my head.

I crawled the remaining ten feet and reached the edge of the cafeteria. I raised my flashlight. Josh's estimate was pretty close. The wall extended upward about ten feet. Beyond that, I saw more beams continuing across.

I lifted myself up, standing vertically next to the wall. The stiffness in my legs and knees hurt. Using my arms, I grabbed on to the next set of risers I could reach and went up another five feet. After repeating that once more, I found myself above the ceiling in the cafeteria. I crawled along the beams again, listening for voices.

43

I heard mumbling as I held onto the beams.

With the ceiling tiles a few inches below me, I reached down and eased the edge of one back. I hung just over the stage. Leaning off the beam, I saw further into the cafeteria. Jax and Niki sat in chairs with their backs against a long table. Once upon a time, school children would've lined that table with their lunch trays in their hands. Both Jax and Niki had their arms bent behind them. They struggled against their restraints.

"Stop trying," Silas said. The stage curtain obstructed my view. "The show will start soon enough."

"Why not just kill us and go about your day?" Jax shouted.

"It shouldn't be much longer before Michael's here. After all of my children you have killed, I'd prefer to look into your eyes as I turn him. I want to cherish the look on your face, having come so close so many times." I heard Silas's footsteps as he marched along the stage. "I'd love for you to watch as you lose another member of your team. I'm going to turn Michael, and then her. I'll turn the big guy in the gym next. All while you get to watch. And for my finale..." He paused as if relishing the thought. "My finale will be to turn you and let you hunt the cripple.

"You and your team have been a pain in my ass for too long. You'll be my new lieutenants. A true night crew."

"The Council will send another team," Niki said. "They'll send every team to snuff you out like the vermin that came before you."

"Council? What Council?" Silas laughed. "You say the word like it should send shivers up my spine. The Council is finished. Don't think that I've made the same mistakes as the 'vermin' before me."

I leaned back onto the beam and continued my crawl. I needed another ten feet before I hung just above Silas. The difficult part would be timing it for when he was right underneath me. The only advantage I had was the element of surprise. I moved a hand down the beam, then another, pulling myself along.

After passing over five more ceiling tiles, I listened again. Silas's muffled voice grew louder. I had to be closer. Slowly, I leaned over and reached for the tile again.

As I did, my foot slipped off the beam. I started to fall. Quickly, I grabbed the beam tight with both my hands. I swung underneath the iron beam, dangling an inch above the ceiling tile. For an instant, my heart and breathing stopped. I stayed there frozen as if I was part of the structure. Everything could've ended at that moment.

Listening, I still heard Silas's voice chastising Jax and Niki. I gripped the beam and brought my chest to it. I eased myself back to the top. It may have been unusually cold outside, but in here, sweat poured from my forehead onto the beam, leaving puddles in the dust.

I brought one hand to my jeans and dried it off, followed by the other. Again, I reached for the corner of the tile and eased it up.

Silas stood just underneath me, lecturing his captives.

I steadied myself before sliding my legs forward and placing my butt on the beam. My feet bent under it, hovering an inch above the ceiling tile. I had to keep my back crouched so as not to hit the roof above me. I grabbed the machete in my belt and slid it out.

Breathe.

I took a deep breath and exhaled. I grasped the hilt of the machete with both hands. Through the edge of the tile, I kept an eagle eye on Silas. I took another deep breath in and exhaled.

With the machete tightly clutched between my hands, I eased myself forward and braced for impact.

The ceiling tile gave no resistance as I fell through it. Silas stood directly underneath me, and the machete aimed directly toward his head ready to bury into it. With the blade inches from him, I knew I had him.

But then he disappeared from underneath me, and I stopped falling. I stayed suspended in midair and couldn't breathe. Silas's outstretched arm held me high above him with his hand wrapped around my throat.

The machete fell from my hands and rattled across the stage floor.

Still holding me above him by the neck, Silas turned to Jax and Niki. I saw them sitting in their seats, violently struggling to free themselves from their bonds and help me.

I struggled as hard as I could to free myself from Silas's grasp. With both hands, I tried to pry his fingers away from my neck. All I managed to do was scratch at my own throat. His grip was so tight, not even a finger would slide between my neck and his hand. I kicked his stomach, but each impact had no effect on him.

"Look who's arrived!" he shouted to them. "I've been waiting since I heard you almost fall off the rafter. Michael the Savior couldn't resist the temptation of saving his friends."

Silas bent his arm, bringing my face close to his. I stared into his burning red eyes and smelled the stench of death on his breath. With a sudden movement, he tossed me across the stage as if I was a rag doll. I slid along the floor and collided with a stack of folding chairs on the far side.

My head banged against them, and stars erupted in my vision. How many more times could I take a blow to the head before brain damage set in? Beyond the stars, my vision blurred, and everything appeared in tunnel vision. Jax and Niki still struggled to help me, but their restraints kept them securely fastened to the table and chairs.

Through the tunnel, I saw motion at the back of the cafeteria. The sound of a door slamming shut echoed off the walls. Had Silas's half a dozen friends joined us already?

"Silas," Thomas yelled.

I glanced up and saw Silas's attention redirect from me. He turned to the sound of Thomas's voice. I struggled to bring myself out of the tunnel and regain my focus. After a few blinks and a head shake, I succeeded.

Thomas stood just beyond the tables on the far side of the cafeteria. He came in from the kitchen door, the same one Martin and I made our way through when we first stumbled upon Silas's sanctuary. Thomas appeared to be covered in blood. His long jacket still flowed around him. Other than the blood, though, he looked untouched.

"Welcome, Thomas," Silas responded. "You're just in time. I should've known you'd be smart enough to get out of my trap."

"Pumping silver into the library? Yeah, you'd have to do better than that. The moment I saw the air shimmer, I escaped outside using the fire exit in the back of the library."

While Thomas had Silas's attention, I rose to my feet. The world spun around me, but briefly closing my eyes, I forced it to stand still. I inched my way forward.

"Speaking of the outside," Thomas continued. "Don't count on betas as a backup. That's insulting."

Silas smirked and gave a slight chuckle. "I hoped the silver would've given them the upper hand. It's fine. After I finish here, I'll make more."

He raised his hand and pointed a finger at Thomas. He gave it a slight wiggle and a look of minor disgust. "Should I assume all that blood is theirs?"

I crept closer. The machete lay on the stage, just a few feet from Silas. I danced my eyes between it and Silas, still inching my way closer. Hopefully Thomas could keep Silas's attention just a little longer.

Thomas marched closer to the stage, throwing a table out of the way as if it was a sheet of paper. "Do I look wounded?"

"You look irrational, brother," Silas said. He kept his eyes trained on Thomas.

As Thomas advanced on Silas, I realized this was my chance. The machete was fifteen feet in front of me. My slow inching morphed into an all-out sprint.

Silas turned his head my direction.

With the machete a few feet in front of me, I dropped to my knees, using my momentum to carry me forward. I grabbed the handle of it as Silas advanced in my direction and bent down to me. With all the force I could find, I drove the blade upward and buried it into his chest. Only the handle remained visible.

Silas stood upright. The force of him rising pulled me to my feet. I stared into his red eyes while still clutching the hilt of the machete. He raised his arms and placed his hands on top of mine.

"You missed the heart," he said as we stared into each other's eyes.

He placed his hands on top of mine, pulling the machete backward. He kept going, forcing me to take a step back, until the blade left his body. He squeezed, and my hands released it. He jerked my arms out to each side. Silas picked me off the ground, suspending me in front of him by my outstretched arms.

Excruciating pain shot through my shoulders. Flashes of white erupted behind my eyes. My chest muscles tried to pull away from bone.

Silas pushed my arms backward, suddenly dislocating my shoulders. I heard the explosion of simultaneous pops. As I screamed in blind pain, he used the momentum to shove me closer and brought my neck close to his lips.

I felt sharp needles plunge into my neck. The twin stings were minor in comparison to the overwhelming ripping pain in my shoulders. I hung there above him, his mouth pressed against my neck, unable to move or fight back.

In the distance, I heard the faint screams of Jax, Niki, and Thomas. The screaming faded. The pain faded. I was helpless to stop the life flowing out of me.

All feeling drained. A sweet painlessness took its place along with the invading darkness. Quickly, the darkness grew and grew, until it became too big to contain and swallowed me.

44

Nothing.

I felt nothing.

Was this Hell? I doubted it was Heaven. If it was, every religion had it wrong.

I floated in eternal nothing, unable to move my broken body. I floated lifelessly except for the small stream of consciousness.

A taste. Taste returned first. Something salty and slightly metallic. It coated my mouth and tongue. The taste started to change. It morphed into sweet. I wanted more. I wanted to binge like a child eating candy or ice cream. I felt the sweet liquor traveling down my throat and filling my stomach.

I felt it.

Feeling.

Feeling returned next. As I consumed the sweet, more and more feeling returned. At first, small sensations fired off, like my arm had gone numb and was slowly waking up. Except instead of just my arm, the sensations reverberated through my whole body.

Electricity danced down my spine. Numbness turned into pinpricks across my body which turned into red hot pain. My broken body felt again, but it felt like it burned.

I tried to turn my head to look at my dislocated shoulders, but it wouldn't move. My chest muscles burned with fire. I felt every injury but had no control to move. I wanted to scream out in pain, but nothing worked.

Trapped.

I was trapped in my head in pain for eternity without the ability to even scream.

Hell. I was floating in Hell.

Pop!

I heard the first pop moments before I realized what it was. The second pop followed shortly after. The pain was indescribable. My shoulders had popped themselves back into place. With the suddenness of it, my whole body convulsed. I took in a deep breath and wailed into the void.

I screamed. I screamed...and I heard it.

Light slowly started to invade the eternal void. The burning subsided, and the pain slipped away with the darkness.

My eyes opened.

I saw broken ceiling tiles above me. I saw dust particles in the darkness above the ceiling tiles. Colors swarmed and floated. Crisp sharp colors I'd never noticed before.

Inside of me, I felt a rumble. Hunger rose, but like nothing I've ever felt before. My whole body craved the sweet liquor that brought me out of the darkness. I needed more of it.

That smell.

I smelled it first. It was here. I had to find it. Where was it?

With one kick, I flew to my feet. Every muscle fiber in my body vibrated with energy. Every nerve ending stood at full alert. The slightest movement of air sent ripples cascading through my senses. My body felt like someone turned all the sensors to one hundred.

A wave of massive hunger hit again. A feeling of unquenching thirst rode the hunger wave. It only wanted one thing: more of what brought me back.

I turned my head and saw Silas standing a few feet from me on the stage. He looked different, though. The whiteness of his skin seemed exaggerated, like an already white T-shirt just freshly bleached again. Beneath the stark white, I saw nothing.

My gaze spun to the voices beyond the stage. The other vampire stood between the stage and the tables. He reminded me of Silas. My eyes fixated beyond the vampire, though, and landed on the two bodies sitting there. Waves emanated from them. The waves pulsated and sent that smell to me. The sweet aroma I craved. It wasn't nothing I saw beneath their skin. I saw red.

I bounded off the stage following the smell, paying no attention to the vampire who stood in the way. He grabbed me as I passed him and tossed me back.

"Michael," he shouted. "I need you to snap out of it."

Silas began chastising him. "Thomas, my dear brother, you are going to deny him his food. Do you not recall how strong and painful the blood lust is? Let the boy eat."

I dove for the table again, but the vampire (*Thomas*) stood in my way. The hunger drove me forward. The smell called to me. I wanted—no—I *needed* what they had. Why didn't he let me by?

The vampire (*Thomas*) tossed me against the stage again, driving me further back.

I shifted my focus from the pulsating waves coming from the bodies (*Jax and Niki*) sitting at the table and concentrated on the obstacle in front of me. He had no pulsating waves of sweet red coming from him or flowing beneath his bleached white skin. He was a marble statue, standing in my way. I charged at him, running my shoulder into his chest at full speed.

He moved back a few inches then stopped. The marble statue wouldn't budge any further.

I kept driving into him, trying to make progress like a football player hitting a blocking sled. My legs continued to pump and push against the tile floor. Suddenly, he spun me around and tossed me to the side.

"Mike, stop," Thomas shouted to me. "Your name is Michael White. You were a sergeant in the army. Grew up here. We are working together to stop Silas from starting a revolution. Try to remember. Break out of the blood lust."

I didn't care what he said to me. I advanced again, and he blocked me out of the way, standing between me and the bags of sweet red liquor (*Jax and Niki*).

"Mike, I don't want to kill you. You saved me, remember? You saved me, and I want to save you. Remember, Mike. Use your gift and remember who you are."

"It's no use, Thomas," Silas said. He still stood on the stage, obviously enjoying the show. "He's going to kill them, and I'm going to turn them. The Council will be gone, and the reign of the Accords is over. Give up."

I rushed at the closest one. I reached a hand out and almost touched her before the vampire hit me again. He bent down and put his shoulder in my stomach. With one quick motion, he propelled me into the air. I landed on my back on the stage and slid past Silas.

I needed the redness. The hunger screamed inside of me. The sound of it deafened everything else.

I jumped to my feet and took a deep breath. My hands clenched, and I closed my eyes as both waves of hunger and anger washed over me. My breathing escalated as I let the anger erupt inside of me.

Brittany's voice exploded inside of my head. "Michael White, stop!"

I opened my eyes and saw her standing in front of me.

45

A cool sea breeze brushed my face.

I stood on a beach next to the coast. My bare feet sunk into the sand. The sun sat directly above me, blasting rays of heat down. I heard the waves lapping against the beach.

Glancing down, I realized I wore a swimsuit and nothing else.

"Mike."

Brittany's voice came from directly behind me. I turned away from the water and saw her. Her red hair tied into a ponytail with a few strands still drifting past her face. She wore her favorite one-piece swimming suit.

"I know this place," I said. "Corpus Christi. We came here this past summer. You came out of the water, teasing me and kicked water all over me."

She smiled. Oh, how I missed that smile!

"Of course you remember," she said. "You never forget anything."

"We aren't really here, though, are we, Brit?"

"Mike, you don't need me to answer that. You know the answer."

Images of the past few minutes passed before my eyes.

"Brit, I'm sorry. I tried. So much has happened in the past few days. I tried to fulfill that promise I made you. I tried to avenge you, but I lost."

"You mean this one," she said. She pointed next to me, and I turned.

In the sand, I saw myself, just home from work. I sat on the ground, and her head rested on my lap. Her chest spasmed as blood poured from the wounds. I cradled her head in my arms, and tears fell from my face onto hers.

The me standing up turned to Brittany. "Don't make me see that again," I begged her. Tears flowed.

"Don't die on me," Memory Me said. "Hold on, baby. Hold on. The ambulance will be here soon. Don't leave me."

She coughed up blood, and her body shook briefly.

"Brittany, stay with me. I promise you, Brit, I will find who did this and make them pay. Everything'll be okay. You're going to be okay. I'm going to be okay."

Her body spasmed again. A blood bubble emerged from her nose, then receded back in.

"Brittany? Brittany!" Memory Me screamed.

The real me turned and stared at the Brittany standing in front of me. "I see you die every time I close my eyes. Why show me again?"

"Because as good of a memory as you have, you forgot your promise."

"Forgot my promise?" I yelled back at her. My anger started to show, and my voice grew loud and direct. "I've been fighting since your funeral to do exactly that promise. Find who did that to you and make him pay."

"You found him."

"But he beat me, Brit. He killed me and brought me back as a vampire. I didn't make him pay."

She took a deep breath and blew it out quickly, obviously frustrated with me. "You are so dense sometimes. You told me you are going to be okay. I don't care about the rest of that. That was a promise you made to yourself. The only part I cared about is when you said you are going to be okay. I knew then I could let go of the pain I was in. I could be at peace because you would be okay."

Those words hit me hard right in the middle of the chest. Since her death, I'd done everything but be okay. I avoided going through the stages of grief, wallowing between Camp Denial and Camp Anger. If I was honest with myself, some Camp Bargaining mixed in there. I'd been fighting and fighting to get my revenge because I thought that was my promise to her.

"Brit, I'm so sorry. I'm not okay without you. I'm in so much pain, and there's no turning back."

"Mike, you can control this. You're strong. You were before this, and you still are. This mission isn't over. You're fighting for more than just me, now. You have the power to end this, so do it."

"Brit, I'm a monster, now."

She scoffed. "You aren't a monster. Look at the difference between Thomas and Silas. A monster is what you make of it. Serial killers are monsters, and yet they're human.

"There are some hard times ahead, and your friends need you more than I do. More than you need me."

"Will I see you again?" The question hurt to ask.

She shrugged and gave me a smile.

"Are you really here?" I asked her. "Have you been here with me through all of this, or are you just up in here?" I tapped my head as I asked.

Her smile broadened. "Do you believe I'm here, Mike? If so, then I am. Now, control yourself and end this. You are so strong, you know. Silas truly fucked up turning you. Go kick his ass."

46

As quickly as I arrived at the beach, I found myself back on the stage. The hunger still burned, but I redirected the anger that swelled along with it.

With my fists clinched, I turned my head from Thomas, who stood on the ground level, to Silas, standing on the stage near me.

Memories of Brittany on the beach, the wind blowing the few loose strands of red hair across her face, the water hitting the shore, her smile, flashed before my eyes like billboards. "You took Brit from me," I said.

Silas turned his attention away from Thomas and looked at me. Realization crossed his face. I was fighting the blood lust.

I kept on. "You took her from me, and you turned me into this." I brought my hands down the front of my body. "You hoped I would be an ally in your revolution."

"I made you powerful," Silas said.

"You preyed on children, and when you found a scared little boy who you sensed a power in, you took advantage of him. You waited for me to grow up and be happy, so you could take away my happiness. You took her from me."

Silas's expression turned to anger as well. "You pestilent little ass. I gave you power. Don't let a hint of humanity weaken what you are capable of."

"Weaken me? You're wrong, Silas. That hint of humanity is a fire inside of me. Without that, I'd lose Brittany forever, and that's not acceptable to me."

"If you won't join me, then you can die all over again."

Silas barreled toward me insanely fast, but I saw him move. I felt the air change as the muscle fibers in his body began to twitch. My senses picked up everything.

Silas drove his fist at my head as he lunged my direction, but I stepped out of the way. He passed inches from me. When he did, I hit him in the back as hard as I could. He flailed forward before spinning around to hit me. I blocked his arm, grabbed it, and tossed him over my shoulder.

His fist hit the top of the stage, cracking it. His eyes burned red with anger.

I stood a few feet from him. I found peace in the images of Brittany and me laughing on our wedding day or sitting on top of Enchanted Rock together watching the sunset.

Silas rose to his feet and charged again. I brought my arm back and saw the spot I was aiming for: the tear left by the machete. As Silas reached me, I punched forward with all my new power, driving my hand into his chest, right next to the machete mark, and out the back of his chest. I held his heart in my hand.

"I didn't miss the heart this time," I told him. I stared into his glazed-over eyes as I ripped my hand back through his body.

Without my hand buried in his chest holding him up, Silas fell to his knees.

I walked over to the machete still on the stage floor, picked it up, and marched back over to Silas still on his knees. I stood behind him and grabbed his hair. I pulled it down toward the floor, exposing the front of his neck to the air. I raised the machete above my head and brought it down as hard as I could.

Before the blade hit his neck, my arm came to an abrupt stop. I spun my head and saw Thomas gripping my arm.

"You've done your part," he said solemnly. "I created this beast. It's for me to finish."

Every fiber in my body wanted to be the one to slice through Silas's throat. I wanted to put the final blow to the dying vampire. Some ounce of humanity still buried inside of me, though, knew my part was over. I relaxed the arm holding the machete, let go of Silas's hair, and stepped back.

Thomas grabbed the blade from my hand as I fell to my knees, nothing left inside of me.

"Once upon a time, we were brothers. I pray that whatever afterlife comes next, we get to be so again. Goodbye, Benjamin." With a quick swing of the machete, Silas's head rolled to the edge of the stage.

47

On my knees with the headless body of my wife's killer in front of me, I lowered my head. I hoped a huge weight would lift off my shoulders with Silas dead. It didn't. Everything still felt heavy.

I raised my head and peered out across the cafeteria. The air appeared to sparkle with dust particles. Smells jumped out, and I noticed things I never had before. I knew there were three dead rats decaying above us.

Niki stood up at the table rubbing her wrists, and Thomas ripped the bindings away from Jax's hands. He also stood rubbing his wrists.

Watching them, I felt starving again. The smell of their blood swam through the air. I doubled over.

Thomas ran to me. With his fingernail, he dug a gash into his arm, drawing a line of blood. "Drink, before it hits again." He waved his arm at the same level as my head.

I grabbed his arm and buried my face in it. I sucked as hard as I could. His blood tasted stale. Nothing like the sweet aroma coming from the other two. It also flowed very slowly. I drew it into my mouth as quickly as possible. The deep hunger pains subsided but didn't go away completely.

"This will help take the edge off," Thomas said, "but we'll need to get you real blood soon. If not, the blood lust will hit again and worse."

After another minute of what felt like drinking through a clogged straw, Thomas pushed me away. Anger welled up inside of me, and I glared at him. Jax and Niki, slowly approaching us, paused.

"It's okay," Thomas said. "Mike, look at me." He snapped his fingers in my face. "Look at me."

"I am looking at you," I said through clenched teeth.

"I mean through your human eyes, not the red ones."

When he said that, I realized that when my anger flared up, colors had become more intense. Where he snapped his fingers left trails in the air. I closed my eyes and took a deep breath. The taste of Thomas's blood still lingered in my mouth. With each breath, the taste stayed ever present. Finally, I opened my eyes. The trailing movements in the air disappeared, and colors fell back to their normal hue.

Jax turned to Niki. "Head to the gym. Nate is still in there. We'll be right behind you if you don't find a way to get him out."

"What about Scott?" she asked.

"He's dead," I somberly said. "He came after me in the hallway. I wish there would've been another way, but..."

"I know," Jax said. "We all do. Niki, also find the comms. Josh has probably called in the army by now."

"Silas crushed ours," she told him.

"Mine is in the library," Thomas said while still standing in front of me. "On a bookshelf when you walk in."

Jax hopped onto the stage and came over to me. I sensed hesitancy in his step as though he approached a barking dog.

Still sitting on the floor, I curled my knees into my chest and wrapped my arms around them. I thought about the scared boy who had wandered in here so many years before. I found myself gently rocking back and forth.

When Jax reached my torso, he touched my shoulder without saying anything. I resisted the urge to drive my teeth into his hand. If it wasn't for Thomas's appetizer meal, I probably would have.

Finally, I looked toward both Thomas and Jax and asked, "What happens, now?"

"Well," Jax said, "first, we're going to free Nate and let Josh know what happened. Then Thomas is going to help you get what you need."

"And after that?"

"After that..." Jax said. He turned his head up for a few seconds, thinking. "After that, we'll figure out things together."

48

Standing on the hilltop, I noticed the air wasn't as cold anymore. Normal October weather seemed to have returned. Tombstones dotted the hillside below until the graveyard flattened out into a sea of headstones. Tents littered the area. For a quiet, small town, the number of funerals over the past week was unheard of.

Forty-three people died at the Club Starlight "fire," including Detective John Jennings. That asshole was given a ceremony with all the bells and whistles of a hero. The news station showed it on television, and he was posthumously given a medal of bravery for the lives he saved. What a crock of shit! Austin—I mean Intel—definitely knew how to spin a story.

An anonymous tip informed authorities about the skeletons of children at the old school. I figured the place would swarm with national media over something like that. Instead, even that was brushed away. The bodies were removed and quietly buried in a cemetery an hour away in the middle of nowhere. I guess that was one way to keep secrets buried. A joint group of the school board and city council voted unanimously to destroy the building in a very late evening emergency meeting.

Missing persons flyers still hung on poles and on billboards. I imagined in a matter of weeks they would disappear. Those who were impacted would hold their funerals, and everyone else would tell campfire stories of the time that children went missing. My heart hurt for those who lost loved ones, but at least I knew their specific monster would never strike again.

I heard leaves crunching behind me as a sweet aroma approached.

"How is it?" Jax asked as he joined me on the edge of the hill.

"Surreal," I said.

"Not every day you get to watch your own funeral."

I nodded in agreement.

At the bottom of the hill, next to where Brittany was buried, a casket hovered above the ground waiting to be lowered. A handful of mourners, the neighbors and coworkers I would never see again, showed up to say their goodbyes. Concentrating, my new heightened senses allowed me to hear my own eulogy.

"The church service was nice," Jax said. "Would've been a little harder to stay hidden in the small church."

"Who's in there?" I asked, pointing toward the casket.

"Intel used the body of a John Doe. The story of you dying from a broken heart made for a great obituary."

"I didn't tell you, but Brittany just wanted me to find a way to be okay after she died. I thought she wanted me to avenge her and kill Silas. Being a part of this...being this...I didn't want to be involved with this forever but look at me, now. Permanent, card-carrying member of the Night Crew."

Jax gave a slight laugh. "Speaking of that, your card should be in the mail any day, now."

"Thousands of out of work comedians, and here we are." I gave a smile.

Down below, those who came to tell me their goodbyes walked past the casket.

"Thomas told me your training's going well," he said, changing the subject. "He said you show excellent control, and your strength already rivals that of decades old betas. You'll be an alpha before long. Silas must have felt your inner strength years ago."

"And look where it's gotten me!" I turned to him. "Instead of moving on, growing old, and eventually having a coronary from eating too many hamburgers, I'll never change. This is it for essentially eternity."

"Or you could change the world."

"I thought it's the Council's job to make sure we don't change the world, just protect it."

Jax took a deep breath. "Speaking of that... The Council has disappeared."

"The entire Council? How do you misplace an entire Council?"

"According to Intel, they've all dropped off the grid. Silas said he wasn't making the same mistakes as others. We don't think he was working alone. There may be co-conspirators on the Council itself."

"What's being done?" I asked Jax.

"That's one of the things I need to talk to you about," Jax said. "When you're ready, Thomas will have a new assignment. He's going to be part of the team rooting out the conspiracy."

"When I'm ready?"

"Yes," Jax answered. "You'll need to be ready because I've been tasked with it also."

"What's happening to the Night Crew? Niki taking it over?"

"I asked her," he said. "She turned me down. She told me after almost losing Nate in the gym, she didn't want it. I think the two of them may be nearing the end of their penance."

"Penance? What are they paying a penance for?" I asked.

"That's a story you should ask them one day."

"If not Niki, then who?" I knew what he was going to say before I even asked the question.

"You, Mike. That's why we need you ready. Nate, Niki, and Josh all agreed. The Night Crew is yours."

I watched as my casket was lowered into the ground. Sergeant Michael White was dead. In his place stood a vampire, a creature of the night, charged with protecting people from other monsters and hunting them if necessary.

I am the Night Crew.

Acknowledgments

I have a few people I need to thank for this book being a reality.

First, I'd like to thank my wife, Terri. She's my first reader and editor and gives the most scathing critiques. All of it helps make each book better than the one before it.

I'd also like to thank my parents, Marshall and Debbie Ricks, who I dedicated this book to. As a child, they constantly encouraged me to pursue the things I love and am passionate about. Unfortunately for them, that ended up being writing horror, watching scary movies, and reading horror books. But, hey, here we are.

Thank you, Joe Mynhardt, Jaime Powell, and the entire team at Crystal Lake Publishing for making this book the very best it could be. You had an uphill task trying to tweak and tailor it into perfection, but it turned out amazing. Far better than I could've ever imagined.

Thank you, Christian Bentulan, for the amazing cover art.

And as always, thank you, constant reader, for spending some time inside my head. You were great company. I hope you enjoyed reading this as much as I enjoyed writing it.

Until next time.

About the Author

Brad lives in Central Texas with his wife and a house full of teenagers. A life long horror fan, Brad pulls inspiration from both classic literature like Stoker and Poe and modern works like Stephen King and Clive Barker. Although new to the publishing world, Brad has always loved to write and tell stories. His debut novel, a supernatural thriller titled "Fear Not The Dead", came out in July 2024.

THE END?

Not if you want to dive into more of Crystal Lake Publishing's Tales from the Darkest Depths!

Check out our amazing website and online store or download our catalog here.
https://geni.us/CLPCatalog

We always have great new projects and content on the website to dive into, as well as a newsletter, behind the scenes options, social media platforms, our own dark fiction shared-world series and our very own webstore. Our webstore even has categories specifically for KU books, non-fiction, anthologies, and of course more novels and novellas.

Readers…

Thank you for reading *The Night Crew*. We hope you enjoyed this novel. If you have a moment, please review *The Night Crew* at the store where you bought it.

Help other readers by telling them why you enjoyed this book. No need to write an in-depth discussion. Even a single sentence will be greatly appreciated. Reviews go a long way to helping a book sell, and is great for an author's career. It'll also help us to continue publishing quality books.

Thank you again for taking the time to journey with Crystal Lake Publishing.

You will find links to all our social media platforms on our Linktree page. https://linktr.ee/CrystalLakePublishing

Follow us on Amazon:

MISSION STATEMENT

Since its founding in August 2012, Crystal Lake has quickly become one of the world's leading publishers of Dark Fiction and Horror books. In 2023, Crystal Lake officially transitioned into an entertainment company, joining several other divisions, genres, and imprints, including Torrid Waters, Crystal Lake Comics, Crystal Lake Games, Crystal Lake Kids, and many more.

While we strive to present only the highest quality fiction and entertainment, we also endeavour to support authors along their writing journey. We offer our time and experience in non-fiction projects, as well as author mentoring and services, at competitive prices.

With several Bram Stoker Award wins and many other wins and nominations (including the HWA's Specialty Press Award), Crystal Lake Publishing puts integrity, honor, and respect at the forefront of our publishing operations.

We strive for each book and outreach program we spearhead to not only entertain and touch or comment on issues that affect our readers, but also to strengthen and support the Dark Fiction field and its authors.

Not only do we find and publish authors we believe are destined for greatness, but we strive to work with men and women who endeavour to be decent human beings who care more for others than themselves, while still being hard working, driven, and passionate artists and storytellers.

Crystal Lake Publishing is and will always be a beacon of what passion and dedication, combined with overwhelming teamwork and respect, can accomplish. We endeavour to know each and every one of our readers, while building personal relationships with our authors, reviewers, bloggers, podcasters, bookstores, and libraries.

We will be as trustworthy, forthright, and transparent as any business can be, while also keeping most of the headaches away from our authors, since it's our job to solve the problems so they can stay in a creative mind. Which of course also means paying our authors.

We do not just publish books, we present to you worlds within your world, doors within your mind, from talented authors who sacrifice so much for a moment of your time.

There are some amazing small presses out there, and through collaboration and open forums we will continue to support other presses in the goal of helping authors and showing the world what quality small presses are capable of accomplishing. No one wins when a small press goes down, so we will always be there to support hardworking, legitimate presses and their authors. We don't see Crystal Lake as the best press out there, but we will always strive to be the best, strive to be the most interactive and grateful, and even blessed press around. No matter what happens over time, we will also take our mission very seriously while appreciating where we are and enjoying the journey.

What do we offer our authors that they can't do for themselves through self-publishing?

We are big supporters of self-publishing (especially hybrid publishing), if done with care, patience, and planning. However, not every author has the time or inclination to do market research, advertise, and set up book launch strategies. Although a lot of authors are successful in doing it all, strong small presses will always be there for the authors who just want to do what they do best: write.

What we offer is experience, industry knowledge, contacts and trust built up over years. And due to our strong brand and trusting fanbase, every Crystal Lake Publishing book comes with weight of respect. In time our fans begin to trust our judgment and will try a new author purely based on our support of said author.

With each launch we strive to fine-tune our approach, learn from our mistakes, and increase our reach. We continue to assure our authors that we're here for them and that we'll carry the weight of the launch and dealing with third parties while they focus on their strengths—be it writing, interviews, blogs, signings, etc.

We also offer several mentoring packages to authors that include knowledge and skills they can use in both traditional and self-publishing endeavours.

We look forward to launching many new careers.

This is what we believe in. What we stand for. This will be our legacy.

Welcome to Crystal Lake Publishing—Where Stories Come Alive!

THANK YOU FOR PURCHASING THIS BOOK

www.ingramcontent.com/pod-product-compliance
Lightning Source LLC
Chambersburg PA
CBHW070416310726
48977CB00003B/717